KILLIN' A LORD OF THE LEVEE

Mathilda Thompson

Cover Art - Christopher S. Thompson

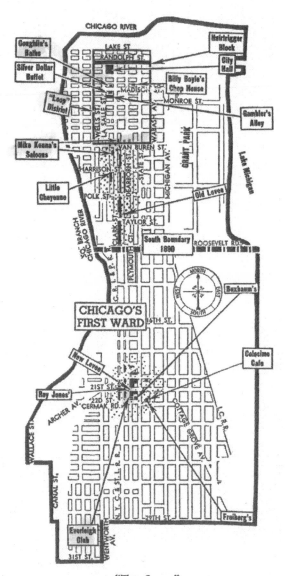

"THE LEVEE"
Chicago's First Ward

Glossary of terms available at back of book.

It must be a good thing to be good or ivrybody wudden't be pretendin' he was. If ye'd turn on the gas in the' darkest heart ye'd find it a had a good raison for th' worst things it done- like needin' the money or punishin' the wicked or tachin' people a lesson to be more careful or protectin' the liberties iv mankind, or needin' the money.

Mr. Dooley -
Finley Peter Dunne

CHAPTER ONE

Steam radiators hissed and clanked.

Sergeant Mike Rafferty's nose twitched and dripped. Reaching for a handkerchief he blew hard, but sounds continued to come to him as from a great distance. He rotated a finger in his ear, hoping that would clear things up, but the noisy bustle around him remained as remote as ever. "That's it, I ain't doin' another fookin' thing," he mumbled, glaring down at the reports on his desk. He felt like going home to bed, and with that thought plus the fact that it was warm in the office, he started to nod off.

"Are you asleep? Can't you hear me?" exclaimed his partner. Mike finally looked up to see Sergeant Karl Weber looming over him, disgustingly full of vigor, and moving up and down on the balls of his feet as if all the cold and drizzle outside didn't matter to him in the least.

"Steele's sending us out." Mike groaned at this new assault on his condition. "He's gotten a tip that Bob Scott's back in town and is hunkered down in some fleabag in the Levee." When even the mention of the country's most infamous burglar failed to rouse Rafferty, Weber leaned closer in concern. "What's wrong?"

Mike fended him off. "Stand back. It's down with something I'm comin'. And it's probably contagious," he added dolefully.

"You're acting peculiar, but you don't look as if you're ailing. Besides Steele's given us an order, and we've got to get going before Scott moves on." Karl went to get his hat and overcoat. While his partner dressed to go out, Mike stared at him balefully.

"Still makin' sure Marshall Field and Company show a profit, are you?" he said, as he took in Karl's new mackintosh and matching fedora. He was even pulling on what looked like a new pair of fleece-lined gloves.

Karl said nothing; he just handed Mike his own old overcoat, rather reprehensible derby, and told him to get a move on. While Mike shrugged into his coat, Karl transferred a pistol from his desk drawer to his overcoat pocket.

"Why're you packin'? Scott's never resorted to violence."

"It wasn't you that got shot at by some unknown a couple of months back. I still don't know who it was, so why should I take chances. Besides, we're going to the Levee, and I can still remember those toughs laying into us down there last summer." Mike shrugged and pocketed his own revolver.

Then looking around ruefully for a moment, he bid a lingering farewell to the warmth and the camaraderie of the detective bureau for other detectives had commiserated with him after hearing he was under the weather. Still reluctant, he nevertheless followed Weber out into the corridor, past the Health Department (where he felt the urge to turn in) then went down the stairs through the usual hangers-on in the lobby (seasoned at this time of year with a handful of the homeless wanting the bit of warmth the radiators were producing), and out of the building into a cold wet November day. "So, who called in the tip?"

"The desk clerk at Scott's hotel."

"Are we walkin'?"

"Why not, it's close enough. Anyway, the cable cars are packed with the rush hour crowd." Mike nodded agreement. The thought of hordes of folks, packed in like sardines, coughing and sneezing in his face was awful. It would only add to his physical misery-walking was better.

"And how did the desk clerk recognize Scott? Was he flashin' his tattoo? No, I take that back. The idjit has burn marks now what with tryin' to get rid of the tattoo."

"For God's sake, Mike, I don't know the whys and wherefores. We're just checking out the tip."

So, heads bent slightly against the drizzle, the two men plowed silently through the crowds south down La Salle Street, making slow progress against the office workers, mostly male, buttoned to their chins and toting umbrellas as they spilled out of the tall buildings along the thoroughfare. Looking tired, most were heading for a bite to eat before catching cable cars or horse cars back home. For others, lodging was a short walk to cheap rooming houses on the fringes of downtown.

Mike raised his head and glanced toward the well-lit shop windows. Soon those shops would close and the numerous salesclerks would add to the crush of folks on the street. The hammering and shouts of the men putting up still more of the city's skyscrapers had already ceased, construction having shut down for the day. Newsboys yelling the latest extras finally tempted Karl into stopping for a paper. He did glance at the headline briefly before slowly folding then carefully easing it into the pocket of his coat.

During the pause, Mike watched someone leap off a cable car with a conductor, head thrust out of the door, shaking his fist, roundly and loudly damning the fellow for hitching a free ride. The car moved on, the conductor unable to leave his post to chase after the miscreant. A traffic cop looked up briefly before resuming his conversation with an attractive young woman. A stout gentleman venturing to ask directions was given short shrift and a brief reply.

At last, the two detectives moved on, leaving behind the grand hotels, the stores with their enticing displays, the finer restaurants, and the towering office buildings to enter tawdrier neighborhoods lined with rooming houses, cheap eateries, sandwich wagons, and pawn shops. The carriage trade had disappeared though plenty of drays still splashed through puddles in the street sending up a filthy spray onto unwary pedestrians. A curse from Weber meant that one of the teamsters had gotten him, in spite of his caution. Then the minor setback forgotten, Karl once again tried to lighten his partner's mood.

"Cheer up, at least the drizzle's keeping down the dust," Karl offered. When Rafferty didn't bother to reply, Karl kept any further comments to himself. And, at last, to Mike's relief, the insistent drizzle stopped. Karl, who'd been watching for the correct address, stopped in front of a three-story hotel, declaring they'd arrived. The establishment wasn't too down at the heels but certainly not top drawer either.

"The Carlton Arms. Now ain't that a fancy name for the place. It looks more like Cockroach Hall."

"Come on, it's not that bad," laughed Karl. "You're sure in a punk mood today, Mike."

"It's easy for you to be sunny. You ain't comin' down with the croup or something," Rafferty said to his retreating partner, who was already energetically heading up the outside stairs. Mike followed at a much slower pace. By the time he entered the lobby, Weber was already interrogating the desk clerk, who was in the process of turning the guest register around so the two detectives could see the signature. From the glint in the clerk's eye, it seemed obvious that he was getting a big rise out of the whole affair.

Probably spends his time reading penny

dreadfuls and the Police Gazette, picturing
himself a great detective, thought Mike, looking
doubtfully at the man. The fellow had an edge to
him apparent in his stiff brush of pomaded hair
and in his sharp nose and chin.

As the two detectives continued to scrutinize
the ledger, the desk clerk was examining them.
He saw a tall, fair, clean-shaven man dressed in a
manner more suited to the business class than the
detective bureau. The other fellow was obviously
Irish. His red hair gave him away. He was
definitely not a fashion place. They were both
probably in their thirties.

"What are you gawpin' at?"snarled Rafferty.

"Sir, I am a student of human nature. Hence
my interest in who comes and goes in this
establishment. And see here, Sergeant," the man
was declaring, "the fellow signed his name, Bob
Scott. I read the papers cover to cover as well. I
know who's who in the criminal underworld."
The sharp chin rose an inch or two. "So as soon
as he signed in, I called you fellas. Real sneaky
he was acting and he's upstairs right now. A real
suspicious character, if you ask me." His voice
rose; he was playing to a larger audience. All ears
in the lobby were turned his direction, all
newspaper pages had ceased turning, one
particularly nosy parker going so far as to part an
obscuring potted palm and peer through the
fronds until a glare from Mike made him
withdraw.

Dismissing the unwanted listeners, Mike
motioned Weber to one side. He hissed angrily,
"Damn it, you know as well as I, that old Bob

Scott wouldn't sign his real name in any guest register. I tell you this is a wild goose chase. Besides, Bob Scott's hardly an uncommon name."

"I agree, but we've got to follow it up so we can tell Steele one way or the other." Turning back to the clerk, he asked, "Is there a fire escape?"

"Of course there is," the fellow declared. Immediate second thoughts came to him, however, and lowering his voice so both detectives had to hang over the check-in desk, he said, "But I do have to say that while it's there, it ain't exactly working."

"What does that mean?" demanded Weber.

"It needs a bit of repair," whispered the clerk.

"Could Scott use it to escape?"

"I wouldn't if I was him. It would probably come down with him."

Mike rolled his eyes heavenward but went along as Weber started for the stairs. The desk clerk made a move to follow but, with a glare, Rafferty motioned him back.

"We don't need that would-be-Pinkerton taggin' along," he told his partner as they trudged up the stairs to the third floor.

Once they reached the third floor corridor, Karl pointed to room 302. As there was no other activity on the floor, the two men took up positions against the wall on either side of the door. Drawing his gun, Weber began pounding on the door at the same time shouting, "This is the police, Bob Scott. We're armed and if you don't open up we'll be kicking our way in and coming in shooting!" He landed a vigorous kick to demonstrate.

"I'm coming, Officer." The door was slowly unlatched, then opened a meager two inches, forcing Weber and Rafferty to push their way into the room. Scott had already stepped back and was standing in confusion near his bed. Though still clad in a business suit of brown wool with a stiff white shirt, he'd obviously begun the process of undressing. Distressed and embarrassed, he was in stocking feet while a highly polished pair of brown shoes stood at attention near the bed. His collar, tie, and watch and chain had been removed and lay on the bureau alongside a pocketbook, cuff links, a tan fedora, and other miscellany. While the two detectives took in the short, stout man and his property, he began declaring his innocence. "I ain't done a thing, honest."

"Are you Bob Scott?"

The man nodded, albeit reluctantly.

"Ah, Jaysus," grumped Rafferty, "our Bob's tall and thin, there's no way he could disguise himself into being short and fat. That fella downstairs has been readin' too many crime reports in the papers. Some student of human nature."

"Let's see your hands," ordered Weber. Trembling and twitching like a pudding, the suspect held them out. Weber looked them over. They were clean and covered in rings.

"No tattoos, no scars," he announced, disappointed. Seeing that the detectives were themselves at a loss, the man began insisting on his rights, and for that purpose drew himself up a few more inches by rising on his toes.

"Ah, shut your gob," growled Mike, "before we think of something else to run you in on. Let's see some identification." The man, whose small spurt of bravado evaporated immediately, began rummaging through his things on the bureau until he found a card which he handed to Rafferty.

"Ah, he's just a drummer, Karl," Mike informed his partner. "Show us the goods to prove it," he ordered. Scott promptly pulled a suitcase out from under the bed, heaved it onto a chair and opened it in order to display the goods inside. It was full of a variety of small packets, bottles, and tins. Weber and Rafferty both leaned closer.

"It's just a lot of nostrums," Weber said in disgust and stood back. Mike leaned closer, suddenly interested.

"You got anything in there for a fella that's getting the croup?" It was Weber's turn to be impatient while Mike listened to the drummer's spiel about each and every cure affected by the various remedies.

"Sears, Roebuck has shown an interest in our medicines. They'll be carrying our products shortly, these ague pills for example. Of course we've just begun showing them here in Chicago, but they've been helping folks in the West and South for thirty years. Even better, here's Doctor Rowland's System Builder and Lung Restorer. It invigorates your whole system; it builds you up.

It's a health-producing pure vegetable extract."
Weber sighed as Rafferty carefully read each
label.

"I'll take the ague pills and give me some of
that restorer too," he finally declared.

"Officer, let them be my gift to you."

"I don't take gifts. I pay my way," said Mike
taking umbrage.

"No offense," said the drummer, backing
away from Rafferty's sharp retort.

"How much?"

"At wholesale, that'll be forty-five cents."
Mike counted out the coins, pocketed the
remedies, and to Scott's relief, turned and left,
but not before Weber, though not too profusely,
apologized for the intrusion.

Going down the stairs, Karl, out of sorts
himself now, groused, "Those things won't be a
bit of help, you know."

"I suppose that's a bit of wisdom from your
brother the sawbones?" Weber nodded. "Well, he
ain't here, is he? Meanwhile, I got these,"
retorted Mike, patting his pocket. "By the way, I
think we ought to give that wannabe Pinkerton
downstairs an earful for wasting police time."

"We can tell him he was wrong, but why
discourage him? Maybe next time he'll be a real
help. By the way, as long as that drummer was
offering his nostrums free of charge why didn't
you take him up on it? It would have given you at
least the price of a meal?"

Looking at his partner as if he'd suggested a
felony, Rafferty retorted, "I suppose that's
wisdom according to Karl Weber. Well, it just

ain't my way of doing things and I ain't in the mood to argue." Weber sighed and dropped the subject. He'd made other suggestions for improving one's financial condition by using insider knowledge and friendships with City Council members which Mike had sternly rejected.

"Listen, Mike, since you're under the weather, I'll put in the call to Steele and then head for home. I suppose you'll be doing the same?" Weber looked at his partner with more concern now that his attention wasn't on something else.

"Probably, yeah."

"I'll be heading north. See you tomorrow," he called out to Mike who was still standing undecided in front of the Carlton Arms.

"Maybe," was Rafferty's glum reply as he began walking in the opposite direction. He stopped at a corner and stood looking toward the string of saloons which lent the darkened neighborhood its most cheerful sounds and brightest colors. He noted the fact that far fewer pedestrians than usual were in the streets. Certainly women were almost non-existent, this not being an area of the slightly more upscale concert saloons. Only a few of the usual kids with buckets were out to get dad's nightly ration of beer at the barroom door. The cold and rain, he surmised, had driven everyone indoors. Even the usual complement of rowdy boys was missing. He continued to stand hesitantly until jostled by a couple of patrons, still full of alcoholic warmth and exuberance, departing one of the saloons.

"Sorry fella," one of the men called back over his shoulder as his friend urged him to get a move on or they'd miss their streetcar. A solitary female, covered in tawdry finery, walked by, paused, and looked hopefully into his face. Seeing no welcome there, her mouth turned down; she shrugged and moved on.

It started to drizzle again, a cold November drizzle with nothing pleasant about it. Rafferty sneezed and shivered. "Jaysus, I feel like shite," he mumbled aloud. Every bone in his body seemed to be aching, his nose was dripping again, and now his throat was beginning to feel raw. He couldn't face the long ride home on an indifferently heated streetcar, moving along at no more than a snail's pace. Not without a pick-me-up, not without somethin' to put a bit of fire in me belly. As an after-thought he added, and something to wash down them ague pills. So with sudden decision he headed toward a familiar saloon, the best on Harrison, one of Patrick Boylan's places, the flagship of the line in fact, down in the First Ward Levee.

The noise level immediately assaulted Rafferty's ears as he competed for entry with other men, also exchanging the chill outside for the comfort of the saloon. Various smells assaulted his nose, the beer, the booze, and the cigars penetrating even his faltering senses. As Rafferty leaned forward against one end of a long mahogany bar that ran almost the entire length of the room, a tall, burly barkeep, whose mustache displayed considerable virtuosity, asked, "What'll ya have?"

Rafferty looked over the stock behind the bar. He saw the usual tasteful medley of lemons, plenty of neatly stacked glasses, an endless array of whiskey bottles, and to give the bar a bit of class, muscatel, sweet Catawba, port, and sauterne. Mike shook his head at those.

"Gimme a shot of the Irish," he finally declared.

Just as the barkeep turned to reach for a bottle and a glass, a voice boomed from the back of the room.

"Michael Francis Rafferty! Back here, Michael, in the back of the room."

Why it's Pat Boylan himself, thought Mike, his face crinkling into a smile. And he strode at once to the back of the room where the war lord of the ward, Alderman Patrick Boylan was holding court, surrounded by the usual flunkies, a pair of fellas that looked and acted like bodyguards, having an air of menace about them and flanking him like two pillars, as well as a number of petitioners waiting for a helpful word with the great man himself.

"Ah, Michael," Boylan declared, wagging a finger at Rafferty, "it's been a long time between visits. And you, one of me own lads." To one and all, Boylan announced, "This here's Michael Rafferty, nephew of me old pal, Francis Herlihy, that used to own a grand saloon on Archy Road. Sit, me boy, sit. Take a load off. Being with the police, I'm betting you've been on your feet the entire day, runnin' from here to there. Now's the time for a well earned rest.

"Sloan," shouted Boylan to the barkeep that

had taken Rafferty's order, "bring the lad's whiskey here. In fact bring the whole bottle. Rosy," he ordered one of his numerous flunkies, a man with hair even more flamboyant than Mike's, "get a plate and fill it up for Michael here and, mind, it's a full plate." Boylan lowered his voice, but it still carried across half the room. "How's your Aunt Maggie doin'?"

"She's doin' fine, Mr. Boylan."

The two men exchanged bits of political and police information until the plate and drinks arrived. Then Boylan urged Rafferty to dig in, saying, "I've a bit of business that needs doing first. After that, we'll have us a long talk."

Rafferty downed the shot. It hit his stomach, the warmth spreading immediately, giving him a much needed boost. He poured himself another from the bottle and began to pick at the ham and turkey, at the cheese, hard and curling up a bit after a long day of sitting on the counter, and at the hard-boiled eggs. Disgusted by his lack of appetite and the worsening rawness of his throat, he sat back and spent more time observing the Alderman than eating.

Without question, Boylan was a lord of the Levee. Expansive in gesture, patriarchal in appearance, magisterially nodding to one and all, Boylan heard from his petitioners. He dispensed a job here, some charity there, and overall reassured his constituents that, as always, he would be there to take care of his own. Rafferty nodded approval. So it had been with his own uncle. It was Boylan who had helped set up his old pal in business, and when he died, it was

Boylan who saw to it the widow received a hefty sum for the saloon, enough to buy herself, and incidentally her young nephew, a modest home. There was even enough left over, so his aunt, who was not one to shirk work, could set herself up in the catering business. And for that matter, Boylan had set Mike up as well by encouraging him to join the police force and then helping him get into the elite detective division at City Hall.

In spite of the fact that Rafferty still felt like his body was fighting a losing battle with the croup, he enjoyed watching Boylan at work. The man made a handsome figure. He thought of the other politicos in the First Ward. *No, he isn't a runt like Kenna, and he's got more dignity than Bathhouse John. And not just because of his graying hair, beard, and mustache, or his height, but because of his manner.* Mike tried to fit something more to the picture and finally decided that he looked like a Prince of the Church. *Yes, an archbishop at the very least.* He smiled.

Each petitioner did look as if he'd just received a blessing. And with the ring-covered hand extended, petitioners weren't far short of kneeling to kiss it. He'd always admired Boylan ignoring the fact that the man had a considerable reputation for corruption. A corruption exaggerated by the press, thought Mike. Hah, those fellows are always exaggerating the worst about Boylan at the instigation of their wealthy owners. And what would rich fellas like that and their toadies know, or even want to know, about the care Boylan takes of the little fella? He knows what's going on in every corner of his ward, in the whole city for that matter. Even now, sitting here, Rafferty could see men being sent on this or that errand for their boss.

Then losing interest in the activity around Boylan, the meaning of which he couldn't always interpret, Rafferty began looking around the saloon. He knew there'd be games going on somewhere upstairs, games preachers railed about constantly. What the hell, when even old Carter Harrison looked the other way, and him once the mayor, why should he, Michael Rafferty, get righteous over a bit of gamblin'? All the same, Mike felt a twinge of guilt. He sipped slowly at his second glass of whiskey and stared at the men leaning on the bar. He stopped to concentrate on one man in particular. The fellow suspected he'd been spotted and was trying to fold himself up like an unused accordion and insert himself between other heftier souls at the bar. It only made them shove the fellow out into the open. He turned at once and dashed for the door.

Ah, the hell with him. I ain't chasin' after that weasel tonight. I just ain't up to it. But I wonder he's tryin' to work his petty cons in Boylan's place. Mike shrugged and turned his attention toward the pool players in another corner and those deep in conversation at the other tables set around the large room. Some had their noses buried in the free newspapers provided for customers. Recognizing a fellow detective, he nodded, receiving acknowledgment in return. After another desultory stab at the food on his plate, the painting back of the bar caught his eye.

He grinned.

Ah, by God, that's a new one, and it's got to be the best damned painting in any saloon in this town," he murmured as he admired an enormous and blood-curdling depiction of Custer's Last Stand through the smoke of countless cigars. The smoke added realism to the puffs of gunpowder surrounding the Seventh Cavalry. Looking further, he was relieved to see that pictures of John L. still graced the walls even though the great man had lost his heavyweight title to that fancy pants upstart Jim Corbett two months earlier. While reflecting on that sad event, he began sneezing again and his nose started to run worse than ever.

"Was that you, Michael, lad?" demanded Boylan.

Rafferty nodded. "Are you ailing?"

"I think I'm comin' down with somethin'."

"Kevin," said Boylan, addressing a young man who'd been hovering behind the alderman the entire time Rafferty'd been sitting there, "go in the back and rustle up a hot toddy for the boy and ask Mrs. Plotz if she's got any soup she can heat up." He turned back to Mike. "Or maybe some beef tea? We always keep that handy when winter weather settles in."

"Soup's fine."

"Then soup it is. After all, we can't have one of the city's best detectives coming down with croup. Why the crooks'd run rampant without you to protect us. But I have to say this, lad, your nose is as red as your hair." Laughing at his own witticism, he gestured to Mike, "Come over here.

Sit closer so we can talk more easily. You can tell me more about how your Aunty's doin'."

"What I've got might be catchin'."

"I never catch anything, lad. Hell," he said, poking a finger at his chest, "the grim reaper'll have to come after me with a revolver to get rid of this fella." Boylan turned to still another flunky.

"Get me a shot and a buttermilk chaser. Now that's the stuff for what ails you. Remember, beer's fermented and everyone knows whiskey is a good remedy. Hell, it's in most of the nostrums those snake oil fellas sell. And don't drink the water." He shuddered at the mere thought of water. "I've had my share of fish comin' out of the faucet. Lake Michigan is still too easily polluted, lad. It could make you sick." He downed the whiskey he'd been handed then sipped the buttermilk. "'Course you can't be too sure of the milk supply either, but a man's got to take some risks in life, eh lads?" Everyone around the table nodded. Again Boylan motioned Mike to move closer.

Abandoning his plate and picking up his glass and bottle, Rafferty moved to a seat on Boylan's left.

"Tell me about the cases that have kept you too busy to visit an old friend that's always been interested in your welfare."

"Well, Mr. Boylan, you know about the Purcell case, 'cause I talked to you about it when me and me partner were doin' the investigatin'."

"Yeah, it was no surprise you catchin' the fella that did it. The two of you struck me as bein' an able twosome. It's just a wonder you could pin the murderer down to one, what with Purcell's havin' so many fellas that hated his guts. I could even have accepted a conspiracy in his case. But in most cases, I always say, look close to home for the murderin' miscreant because that's where most of the rancor is that's always eating away at folks. I expect you've handled lots of domestics."

Rafferty nodded and blew his nose again. "Too damned many," he finally managed.

"Michael, dissatisfaction with one's lot in life, that's human nature. Now tell me more about your Aunt Maggie."

"Why she's just fine, Sir. You know how she is; she's always got to be working. She started by baking meat pies for the lunch wagons that serve the packing house workers. The pies were so popular, she's putting out a whole line of baked goods and has two ladies comin' in everyday to help her out. She's got her own business goin' and it's goin' good."

"Maggie always was a go-getter. A lot of the success your uncle had was her doing, you know."

Rafferty nodded. "And they took me in as well when the folks died of the typhoid."

After that remark, Boylan sat in silence for a time, evidently reminiscing. Mike left him to it.

"Thinkin' of the old days, I was, lad," he finally said. "We saw a lot of each other in those days. Your Aunt Maggie was a looker. Had a bit of an eye for her meself. But it was your uncle she took to. And your folks they were part of our little circle. Our people came from the same place in the old country you know. Of course your Uncle Frank's folks, they were County Cork people. But hell, being Irish, we all had the same difficulties to face. It was a great shame your folks got carried away so young by the typhoid. A great shame. But at least you had your Aunt Maggie and Uncle Frank to look out for you.

"Ah, we were young and frisky, the lot of us, with no thought of getting old and dying in spite of what our folks went through in Ireland. I've been through a lot of weddings and christenings since then--though lately it's been more funerals and wakes." He leaned closer to Rafferty and the flunkies and petitioners did the same in an attempt to catch his pearls of wisdom.

"But even the hurdles we faced in those days couldn't keep us down. Bead counters and cheap shanty Micks, they called us. Hah, no Irish need apply. Those signs are in the dustbin now. They've got to reckon with us in all the big cities now, eh lad? But we had to work hard in the precincts and neighborhoods. It wasn't an easy climb up the political ladder. I think, though, that we have a natural talent for politics. Look at the Germans. One third of Chicago's German, but do they have a lot of office holders? No, they do not. 'Course they blame that failure on the roughhouse tactics of the Irish gang." Boylan laughed. "Hah, it's just that they've no skill in the game. Politics, why it favors the mixers and the spenders." Rafferty nodded and so, very solemnly, did all the hangers on. Boylan continued recalling the past. "But we had good times as well back then. The dances. The picnics. Of course, we've still got those, and the parades," Boylan went on. He liked to talk and only stopped when Kevin finally approached with the hot toddy.

"Kevin's another of me lads, Michael. Kevin, meet Michael, one of the city's finest. He works out of City Hall. Kevin here's like a good right arm to me," he added, smiling benevolently on that same young man.

As Boylan momentarily turned his attention elsewhere, Mike appraised the young man who'd brought him his drink and found himself being scrutinized in return. Mike grinned and Kevin, ever so slowly and tentatively, returned the smile, but it still seemed as if he didn't quite approve of Mike. Rafferty shrugged. If the fella wasn't wanting to be friendly, well, that was no big deal. But it was good to see the evident solicitude with which he hovered over Boylan. The slim dark-haired young man was well turned out. Weber should see him, mused Rafferty, picturing his partner. The two of them could compete in the best-dressed department. In a dark conservative suit and black fedora, Kevin looked like a priest on "Archbishop" Boylan's staff. In fact, for a bodyguard, thought Mike, he looks downright austere not like that plug ugly guarding Boylan's other side with his loud checkered pants and eye popping flowered vest.

"Ah, here comes the soup," announced the alderman. "Thank you, Mrs. P. This will set the lad up if the toddy doesn't." A stout, taciturn woman with budding whiskers, she set down the bowl of steaming broth and, without a word, returned to her place in the kitchen.

"And never fret, Michael, about goin' home in one of them streetcars and freezing your ass off. 'Cause, I swear, it feels like they take the sides off in the winter when they should be on, and put them up in the summer when they should be off. Anyway, Kevin here will take you in one of my rigs, all properly bundled up and with a hot brick at your feet."

Mike sighed with relief. "Many thanks. Riding them damned things and waiting for me transfer would give me pneumonia for sure." Kevin's mouth, he noted, turned down at the task he'd been given but only momentarily, then he put on a stoic expression again. Can't say as I blame him, thought Mike, it's a nasty night for driving all the way to the west side and back.

A sudden shout from the doorway caused Rafferty to spill a spoonful of soup as well as alerting all the flunkies around Boylan into a defensive stance. Even the alderman's eyes opened wide and Mike could see him tense. A man built like a packing box approached the table, fists flailing at those around him, mouthing threats and hurling accusations. Kevin stepped forward, his hand going toward the inside of his jacket just as Mike rose from his seat, but Boylan waved them both off. He motioned his accuser closer, a big man with such close cropped hair that all the bumps and contours of his head were exposed.

"What's the matter, Knobby? I thought the two of us were friends."

"Ya promised me a job after the election. And didn't I get the votes out for ya? Where's me job? I got a wife and six kids to support as you well know. You've let me down, Boylan, you have. Me what voted for you seven times meself." He pounded so hard on the table with his fist that the glasses clattered and the soup dish slopped over its contents.

"Simmer down and sit down," ordered Boylan. And the man, after some hesitation, sat down heavily in a chair indicated by Boylan. Kevin relaxed and withdrew back behind his mentor and Mike settled back into his seat. He dipped his spoon into his soup, without, however, taking his eyes off the proceedings. The intruder was still taking in great gulps of air, but the situation seemed under control. The noise in the saloon that had abruptly ceased returned to normal, but not before an audible sigh of relief traveled around the room. Glancing briefly at the patrons, Rafferty noted the fact that his police colleague at the far table was also removing his hand from inside his coat where he was doubtless carrying a revolver.

"Now, Knobby, did you get paid for your work at the polls?" mildly asked Boylan.

"Sure."

"So you ain't starving yet, are you?" Knobby shook his head. "And I got a lot of things to be taking care of, ain't I?"

"Well, yeah."

"But you were in my thoughts. I appreciate all you did for me. It just so happens I do have something for you. I just hadn't got around to telling you. So there's really no cause for all this sound and fury now is there? Here I am getting you a good spot, and you come in here scaring my friends and reading me the riot act. That's the last thing I would have expected from a reliable fella like you."

"I'm sorry," said Knobby, who was looking penitent. "I guess it was the wife. She sort of put me up to it. She's been naggin' at me, and I guess I just blew me top. Sorry," he repeated. He was still opening and closing his fists and Rafferty figured that when Knobby got home there'd be one of those domestic brouhahas that he and Boylan had been discussing.

Boylan must have figured the same because he said, "Now, Knobby, I don't want you thinking you should be mad at your Missus over this. She's just worryin' for the kids and that's why she was complainin'. You know how mothers are when it comes to their kids. Now isn't that so?"

"I guess," said Knobby, scratching at his landscape of a scalp to help the thought along.

"Here's a little something to tide you over til you have a payday." Boylan handed over a bill which the big man eagerly snatched. "A beer for the big fella here and a cigar, one of the ten-centers," he called out. "And then get yourself home," he ordered Knobby. "Tomorrow, at nine in the morning, I want to see you at City Hall. There'll be something waiting for you. It should make the Missus proud of you and stop the complainin'." He waved the man away. "Go on, go get your beer and then get home."

Knobby stood up looking no more dangerous than some big slobbering dog wanting to lick his master. Shuffling through the sawdust, he headed for the bar where he was soon absorbed among the other drinkers.

"Brian," said Boylan, turning to the plug ugly at his right, "see that Knobby's Missus gets a load of coal." The man nodded. Mike looked at the man in question. Such a romantic name, he thought, for a fella that should be more appropriately called Spike, Bull, or Knocko, because he looked like a refugee from the prize ring.

Waving a hand, Boylan continued to the men surrounding him, "I saw the lot of you tensin' up but there was never anything to worry about. See, I know all these fellas. I know what makes them tick, and I can handle them all." He laughed. "And I guess the city's got another street cleaner now.

"Michael, you might not think it to look at Knobby, but that man makes a smart scrapper. Around elections, he takes time off from his Missus to keep the bums in line. It's him that keeps the drunks from straying off before the polls open. He brings 'em back when they wander, gives 'em a bit of a knock on the noggin and jams 'em back into their barrelhouse bunks. And he ain't never sold me out yet." Boylan grew serious and leaned in close. "There's them that let themselves be bribed by the corrupt opposition, but not Knobby. Let me tell you, it ain't easy putting in enough ballots to offset the school teacher element out there. Costly too. And there's those in the opposition that resorts to fists and sticks and things. You know that yourself, Mike. You've seen it all. Yeah, as someone once said, 'Politics ain't bean bag.'"

Ah, another fan of Finley Peter Dunne, thought Rafferty, himself a reader of the popular columnist, who'd undoubtedly came up with that particular political insight.

"And lately the crusaders are being heard," grumbled Boylan, "what with the Fair comin' next year, they want to clean up the town so's the visitors don't suffer from shock. Before too many months, I'll be looking under the table when I sit down to a peaceful game of solitaire to see if a policeman in civilian clothes ain't concealed there. No offense, lad. Ah, what the hell, I shouldn't worry, the crusade won't last past the first sprint. The good man only works at his crusade once in five years and only when he has time to spare from his other duties. It's only a pastime for him. But the defense of vice is a business with the other lads, and they nail away at it, weekdays and Sundays, holy days and fish days, morning, noon, and night. Yeah, vice," Boylan laughed. "Why that's what lots of folks will be coming to Chicago to see in 1893 and what they come to see every other year as well. And I ain't the only one with that opinion. Me old pal, Finley Peter Dunne, the reporter, says the very same thing." Rafferty nodded.

Boylan's discourse on the facts of life in Chicago was rudely interrupted when a fist fight broke out at the bar. The barkeeps immediately

closed in from all directions using their bung
starters right and left and soon gave the
belligerents the bum's rush. Kevin and Brian
stayed immobile next to Boylan so Mike didn't
move either. Let the barkeeps handle it, he
thought, damned if I'm up to anything tonight.
And Boylan, hell, he's lookin' as if a brouhaha
happens on the hour, which it probably does.

"Michael, that was just a bit of a tiff. My
beerslingers are up to handlin' it." He saw Mike
glance at Brian and Kevin. "There's another
reason to have those two boys. There's rivalry
here in the Levee. There's them that think I'm the
enemy. In case they get ideas Brian and Kevin
can head them off." He sat back again and
smiled. "Not that I'm worried. Those threats are
mostly a lot of hot air." Mike frowned. "No,
honestly, Michael, I've really nothing to worry
about. Truly, it's a good life owning a string of
places and serving the great city of Chicago on
the city council. Hell, most of them on the
council are barkeeps just like me. Why, if
someone was to stand at the back of the council
chamber and yell, 'Yer saloon's on fire,' the
council room would be emptied in nothing flat."
Smiling he looked around his domain with a
proprietary air. Then suddenly he frowned. "Will
you look at that now. Using the bill I gave him to
be treating the rest of them fellas at the bar. No
wonder the man's penniless and his Missus
grouses. Brian, go over and ship Knobby home
and give him one of them mints. I don't want
more trouble with his Missus." Boylan shook his
head. "Good at the polls, he may be, but feckless

otherwise," he commented, as Knobby was escorted to the door. No sooner was he gone when another party started in to shouting, gesticulating wildly, and staring so intensely up to the ceiling that Mike took a glance upwards himself.

"Damn, here we go again. We're havin' us an unusually lively evening."

"Sloan, get over here," Boylan called out, signaling the barkeep that had served Rafferty initially. When Sloan reached the table, he was immediately reamed out. "You damned fool. Didn't I tell you fellas never ever to serve Donohue anything, not even beer."

Casting a penitent look toward the bar, Sloan apologized, "Ah, boss, we were so busy, I guess we weren't looking too close.

"Yeah, well you should'a been because now someone's got to take the fella home and you can see to it. I don't want him sittin' down on some curb and catchin' his death." The barkeep shrugged and went to do his duty.

Boylan explained the situation to Mike. "See, Donohue, he gets a drink, he starts into seeing things and yelling and prancing about. Though being a good Irish lad it ain't no pink elephants he sees, he's got his own personal pooka. And him born and bred in Chicago. Yeah, he sees a pooka just like he was back in the old country." Boylan laughed. "Ask me what he sees." Intrigued, Mike asked. "A giant horse is what he sees. Seamus he calls it. Isn't that some moniker for Donohue's personal pink horse." He laughed wholeheartedly again before turning his attention elsewhere.

Rafferty nodded and tried concentrating on his soup, wondering if he'd be well enough to show up at work the next day. He groaned inwardly thinking of all the paperwork he'd left undone and reached for the hot toddy again. *The lieutenant will have to put Karl onto it.* He took a sip and smiled briefly at that thought before being consumed by another fit of sneezing.

CHAPTER TWO

Surrounded by those colleagues who were
not out actively pursuing criminals, Weber stood
making rejoinders to what passed for wit in the
detective squad while at the same time wrapping
a package for Rafferty. Spotting the assembled
men, Lieutenant Steele approached.

"Going out to see Rafferty?" he asked.
"Yes, and it's about time I did," said Weber.
"I've got his Benevolent Fund money and he'll
no doubt be wanting it"

"Are you renting a rig?"

"Yes, I've too much to carry on a horse car,
plus it's too damned cold today to be going at a
snail's pace. Anyway, I'll be going on to the
wake after seeing Rafferty."

"It's good you're taking a rig, because if
Rafferty's up to it, I want him to go to the wake
with you. He was planning on coming back to
work in a day or two anyhow and he may as well

start with the wake. You know he'll want to be in on the investigation."

"I'm sure he will."

"Tell him we all want him back on the job. Isn't that right fellas?" The hovering detectives loudly seconded the statement.

Steele laughed. "Tell him we miss having Father Rafferty keeping us on the straight and narrow. Besides, what with the hoodlums pouring into town in anticipation of our Columbian Exposition, we'll need every man." The lieutenant's expression became slightly more harassed.

"Anyone here read the Tribune lately when they included comments from the out-of-town papers regarding crime in Chicago?"

Several hands were raised and Weber nodded as well. "They're really ragging us over that highwayman we haven't caught. As if Detroit and Cincinnati haven't got sandbaggers, footpads, and the like. This reputation we're getting is downright unfair, boys. Unfortunately, a mounted highwayman in this day and age holding up carriages and pedestrians is news,

"Lieutenant." offered Weber, "I'm not surprised the Detroit Free Press and other papers are printing stuff on our Chicago lawbreakers. They want to take the heat off themselves."

"You're right, but it sure puts the pressure on us," other detectives agreed. One voiced the opinion that though the Fair would bring in the money it was bringing every lowlife in the Midwest into Chicago as well.

"Hell," added another voice, "they're even coming in from the East and West coasts thinking they'll have easy pickings."

Now Steele looked definitely unhappy. "You're right and the big cases, they keep happening as well." Then he glanced at the package being assembled. "What did we all chip in for?"

"A basket of fruit to keep him healthy," replied Weber. The lieutenant agreed that was a good idea before returning to his office.

Bundled up against the cold and hefting his packages, Weber stepped out into the corridor where Officer Mulcahy spotted him.

"Now would those parcels be for ould Rafferty? I heard from some of the fellas that you was planning on going out to see him."

"You heard right, these are for him."

"Well, me and the rest of the uniforms here at City Hall, we took up a bit of a collection ourselves, and we'd appreciate you're takin' our gift along with yours. If it ain't too much trouble, that is." He looked Weber up and down, as usual admiring his sartorial splendor, even if his outfit that day was what the well-dressed gent wore in a blizzard. Mulcahy sighed and looked down, taking in his own tight and shiny uniform, which as usual, looked ready to burst its buttons. To his chagrin a big grease spot was also right in the center. He hastily crossed his arms over his chest, then grinned up at Weber who topped him by several inches.

"Anyhow, give the lad our best."

"I'll do that," replied Weber, adding what appeared to be an attractively wrapped bottle of whiskey to his stack.

Considerably later, Weber and his rig turned down the streets to Rafferty's neighborhood. Small frame houses lined both sides, looking as if they'd been stamped out by some construction contractor's cookie cutter even down to the lace curtains in each parlor window. No grand lawns or verandas graced these private homes, but they were newer and appeared substantial for they were all two-storied and had separate stables in the back. And, Weber thought, when spring rolled around again, they'd have their bit of greenery. Now though, the leafless fledging elms shivered pathetically in the cold wind.

Weber began counting house numbers, finally pulling up to the correct address. Mentally, he congratulated himself on having avoided the pits and potholes that lay in wait for unwary travelers on any but Chicago's main thoroughfares--and for having arrived safely at his destination. There was no hitching post, so getting down from the rig, he lowered a weight, tied the horse to that, gathered his parcels together, and ascended the eight or nine stairs to the front door. Setting down his load, Weber gave the door several sharp raps.

"Shite," growled Rafferty, tossing the papers he'd been reading onto the floor. Then for good measure, he rose and kicked them across the room frustrated by what he'd read. It was a useless gesture and he knew it. He went to the bedroom door, flung it open, and called down the stairs, "It's going back to work, I am."

His aunt appeared at once from the kitchen, "Michael Francis Rafferty! It's no such thing you'll be doing. Why, it was at death's door you were. You need more time to recover. I know what's rilin' you but can't someone else be doin' it?"

"None of the other detectives knew him like I did, damn it."

"Don't be swearin', Michael."

"I'm gettin' dressed, Aunt Maggie, and goin' back to work." He reentered his room, slamming the door. Once back in the bedroom, he let loose a string of useless curses until his "damns" were silenced by a knocking at the front door. Looking out, Mike saw a tallish person clad up to the eyeballs against the cold, some sort of fur ball on his head, a muffler wound God knows how many times around his neck, heavy mittens, and to complete the outfit, a pair of overshoes. Racing out of the room and down the stairs before whoever it was could knock a second time, Rafferty opened the door. He stared in astonishment.

"Is it you in there, Karl"? He received a nod. "God, you look like a North Woods grizzly come out of hibernation." There was a sound behind Mike and his aunt came halfway out of the kitchen. "It's just me partner, Aunt Maggie. Come to call."

"Well, show the man in and close the door. We don't want to be heating up the whole street. And for heaven's sake, help the man unwrap."

Mike helped Karl unwind his scarf, took the mittens and cap, at the same time making the introductions.

"Aunt Maggie meet me partner, Karl Weber. Karl, this is me aunt, Mrs. Margaret Mary Herlihy. After a brief swipe of flour-coated hands on her apron, a woman still in her prime and echoing Mike's red hair, though with some strands of grey, extended her hand and gave Weber a hardy handshake.

"Take you friend upstairs, Michael, the parlor's not heated. I'll be bringin' the two of you something warm in a minute. It's like the North Pole out there, young man, and you'll be needin' something to take the chill off."

Karl pulled off his rubbers.

"I wouldn't want to be dripping all over your aunt's rugs," he explained. Retrieving the packages he'd set aside earlier, he followed Mike's lead and went upstairs.

"God, it's cold out there," complained Karl, as he warmed his backside in front of Mike's coal grate. "The wind's blowing off the lake. You should see the lake shore. It's icy, gray, and colder than the heart of a plutocrat being asked for a pay raise. And it's not even winter yet!" That said, Weber began to examine Mike who appeared to be clad in something resembling an Indian blanket with matching wooly slippers on his feet.

"So how are you? Recovered yet? We heard you were at death's door, but you don't look nearly that bad to me."

"I'm not doing too badly though things were nasty for a time. Now, to what do I owe the pleasure of this visit?"

"I came to bring you the money owing from the Benevolent Fund."

"Finally me dues are payin' off," replied Mike, readily accepting the packet Karl offered and immediately found a much larger offering thrust upon him.

"This is something from all your colleagues in the squad. We took a collection and hope this cheers you up. I'm just sorry I couldn't get out here to deliver it sooner," he added as he watched Mike undo the string and paper around the rather ungainly parcel.

"Jaysus, oranges, and at this time of year. That must have set you fellas back." He poked through the basket and besides oranges, pears, and apples saw one exotic looking fruit he couldn't immediately identify. "And what is this?"

"A pineapple."

"I've heard of 'em, but never tasted one. I guess Aunt Maggie'll know what to do with it. And this?"

"Whiskey from the uniform squad at City Hall, given to me this very morning by Mulcahy. The box of chocolates from Gunther's, that's a token of my esteem."

Mike snorted.

"Sure, it is. Got tired of workin' two shifts did you? Not that you don't look fit. Nose looks a bit nipped though."

"It was dammed cold driving out here."

"You rented a rig and drove here? You were lucky not to sink clear through to China."

Karl laughed. Then he took the time to appraise his partner more closely."Like I said, you don't look half bad, Mike. Anyway, early November you were probably better off here than at work. Day was like night downtown. There wasn't a bit of wind and with all the chimneys pouring out black smoke and soot, lights had to be left on all day. You should have seen the poor clerks taking their customers outside to see fabric by daylight, only there wasn't any. Finally a cold wind started up, and we got back to our normal semi-solid atmosphere. The paper said the electric company chimneys were the worst offenders, but with the lights on all day, their profits actually increased. No, the air's better out this way. Believe me, you wouldn't have wanted to inhale that stuff."

"Well, I'm recovered, and I'm comin' back to work soot or no soot. O' course me Aunt Maggie still insists on wrappin' me up," he muttered, looking self-consciously down at his slippers and fingering the woolen wrapping around his neck. His expression grew serious. "It was at death's door I was and she pulled me through so I shouldn't be complainin'. I was pretty bad and that I survived at all was due to her and to Alderman Boylan. The evening I began ailin', he sent me home in his rig wrapped up to me eyeballs and with a hot brick at me feet. Lent me his own buffalo robe as well. That and the hard stuff he offered, saved me. If I'd gone home on one of those fookin', freezin' streetcars,

I believe I would've been finished off. And the next day bright and early, a doctor arrives on me doorstep sent by the good man himself. No quack neither, but one of the better sort. . . Boylan's personal physician. As for Aunt Maggie. With her it's a rosary every night, and I headed the list of requests. Plus there was the broth and the cossetin'.

"Listen I'm blatherin' on and you're still standin' at attention." He waved Weber toward a comfortable armchair near the window. "Sit down and tell me what's new downtown." After a pause, he added, "And don't tell me about the hoodlums comin' to town because of the Fair, or that Philo Durfee's finally been nabbed. I think you know what I want to hear about first."

"I figured you'd heard the news already." Mike nodded, gesturing towards the crumpled papers littering the bedroom floor.

"I heard about it, and read about it and Jaysus, I still can't believe Boylan's gone. Karl, I tell you that was a good man, and the killer's got to be caught. Who's handlin' the case?"

"It was taken out of the hands of the local precinct almost at once, being too big a case, and assigned to us at City Hall. So, it's me, Lieutenant Steele, and Willie that are dealing with it, plus a lot of uniforms doing the more routine running around."

"Jaysus, an Englishman and a German workin' on a case of murder in the Levee."

"Willie's Irish."

"Willie can't tie his shoelaces without help. He only got on the downtown detective squad because his wife's some sort of cousin to some alderman's spouse. . . yeah, a third cousin, twice removed."

Karl smiled and shook his head. He knew Willie's faults, but Mike was exaggerating. Willie was a bit of a clown all right but he followed orders and was patient with the plodding work, though Karl had to admit there'd never be any clever solutions or insights coming out of his head.

"It being Boylan, the pressure's on for this one." Karl shook his head. "Not from the Municipal Voters' League. They're no doubt saying that's one less shady politician. But the City Council members plus his constituents are all hot and bothered. Bathhouse John, Mike Kenna, Johnny Powell, Foxy Ed Cullerton-they're all raising holy hell. That's why I'm going to the wake today."

"Steele's sendin' you to an Irish wake? Who the fook does he think will talk to you? They'll nod politely, stand you in a corner and that'll be that. Of course, you could say the rosary with the ladies; that might get you a few points." Mike paused then stated firmly, "If you're goin' so am I. I was plannin' to go anyway."

"I hoped that would be the case." Karl looked relieved. "In fact the lieutenant wants you there and the rig I've got is a big one. You could wrap up and maybe your aunt could give you a hot brick for your feet." Mike waved the solicitous offers away.

"Never mind that, I want the particulars about the murder. Tell me what you've learned so far." A knock on the door interrupted his request for information. Without waiting for an acknowledgment, Rafferty's aunt walked into the room balancing a tray which she deposited on a table after Mike hurriedly shoved aside some books. With a "help yourself," she left them to it.

"Food's the answer to most problems for Aunt Maggie," said Mike. He motioned Karl to help himself. Before settling back in a chair of his own and putting his feet up on an ottoman, Mike offered to pour some of his whiskey into the tea. Without waiting for a reply, he topped both their cups with a shot.

"Now I'm ready to hear about the whole dirty business," he declared. Between sips and bites Karl told the beginnings of it.

"Boylan was shot in his own saloon. It was late at night, and he was alone. Did you know he had a room over the saloon fixed up as an office, but with sleeping accommodations?" Mike said that he did and Karl continued, "I guess if it was late, he'd camp there instead of going home. That's where he was found. Of course, the entire premises was searched. It's a real rabbit warren of rooms, and he owned two connecting buildings besides. There were gambling rooms next door though it was as clean as a whistle by the time the police went through the place. They didn't find even a stray poker chip, just plenty of empty tables and chairs."

"His business will be up for grabs now, and they'll be fightin' for his City Council seat as well. As to the gamblin', you ain't tellin' me anything I didn't know. I know Boylan wasn't a saint." He leaned toward Karl. "He had at least two bodyguards. Where in the hell were they when he needed them?"

"I suppose you're referring to Kevin Fitzpatrick and Brian Duffy. Boylan sent them home around midnight. That's where they say they were the rest of the night. In their rooming house, that is."

"So when Boylan finally needs them, they were in bed sleepin'. Do they have alibis?"

"After the body was discovered, they were rousted out of bed by Boylan's barkeep, a man called Sloan, plus the local police. It's not too clear exactly when they did turn in though. We'll have to question them again. We've only been through it with them once."

"What's the time of death?"

"In the wee hours, somewhere around two or three in the morning, the deputy coroner thinks. "

Mikes' eyes narrowed in suspicion, "And who was on the job?"

"First Search Masterson," said Karl with an air of apology.

"Yeah, him whose light fingers are making him rich. God knows what he pocketed that could be vital."

"He knows better than to lift something that could be a clue to the police."

Mike gave a derisive snort. "I wouldn't count on it." Then he shrugged. "We can't do anything about Masterson's rushing to be first at the scene. What's done is done. Anyway, you say no one heard anything? The saloon was still open, wasn't it?"

"It was, but the room was sound proof, probably so Boylan could sleep in peace and quiet."

"Was he expectin' anyone?"

"If he was, he didn't tell anybody. He was wearing a nightshirt and robe so he was getting ready for bed. There was a glass of whiskey on his desk, maybe a nightcap."

"There's a woman that lives on the premises. She cooks for the saloon and for Boylan when it's necessary."

"That would be Mrs. Plotz. We talked to her. She was sound asleep or so she says. Her room's downstairs and well away from Boylan's private office."

"Who discovered the body? Shite, it's hard to talk about Boylan like this," groused Mike, shooting his partner an irritated look.

Karl expressed some sympathy before continuing, "Mrs. Plotz discovered the body in the early morning. She was supposed to bring him breakfast but found the body instead. She ran downstairs screaming so one of the day barkeeps, in early to restock, went to investigate. He's the one that put in a call to the local precinct, though probably not until all evidence of the gambling had been cleared away." While Mike waited impatiently for more information, Karl helped himself to another scone and poured more tea. He even took the time to look around the room, and Mike caught his look of surprise at the wall of books.

"Did you think I spent all me time readin' Nick Carter, Penny Dreadfuls and the Police Gazette?"

"Of course not. But that's a lot of books." Weber, who was an avid reader himself, got up to read the titles and authors. "William Butler Yeats and George Moore. Irish writers? And will you look at the magazines: Harper's, Collier's, Century, Scribner's."

"Well, don't think that the Germans have a monopoly on readin'." When Karl reassured him that he'd never claimed they had, Mike said, "It's what I spend me money on, not fine clothes from Marshall Field like another fella I know." Karl put up his hands in a gesture of peace. "Ah, just get on with the case."

"We've been working on lists of folks who saw Boylan that last evening."

"Boylan saw lots of folks every day."

"But that last evening he might have let something drop that'll give us a clue."

"I'm thinkin' the interviewin' will be goin' on til the Last Judgment, Boylan knew so many folks. We need to get a line on his enemies. He told me he had enemies, yet in the next breath, he brushed the whole thing off."

"He did have two bodyguards during the day."

"Yeah, and sent them home at night. Have you interviewed the wife?"

"Steele did that, offering his personal condolences at the same time. She says she doesn't know a thing." Mike's aunt had come in with a fresh pot of tea and overheard the last remark.

"Well, she wouldn't, would she. I couldn't help hearin'," she explained.

"What do you mean, Aunt Maggie?"

"Boylan wasn't a homebody, that I can tell you. Mary Boylan wouldn't have a clue about his business or his politics. He never confided in her about anything."

"You knew Boylan way back when, didn't you, Aunt Maggie? He told me so himself. He said he was sweet on you but you preferred Uncle Frank. Now I thought the world of Uncle Frank but he wasn't what you'd call a political and financial success like Boylan. In fact, didn't Boylan help Uncle Frank start his saloon?" Mike moved to sit on the bed and pointed to his own chair. His aunt seemed please to be asked to sit and talk about what she knew.

"Your Uncle Frank, Paddy Boylan, and I go back to the time of "No Irish Need Apply", she said referring to a ballad popular with the Irish as far back as the 1860s. "He wasn't the financial success then that he became later. No, your Uncle Frank and I both worked hard and saved and put down a hefty down payment for a saloon; but Boylan did help us pick a good location, and he negotiated with the breweries and liquor interests since he was already working in the business. He gave us a lot of good advice."

"You say he took a shine to you, so how come you weren't interested in him when you maybe could have had him. . . or was that just blarney he was handin' me? No offense, Aunt Maggie."

"None taken. No, he wasn't puttin' you on or at least not completely. He hung around me." She sniffed. "He hung around a lot of girls and sweet talked them, tryin' to get what he wanted. But when he married, it was Mary McCarthy, her whose dad owned a butcher shop. . . more than one and blocks of buildings besides.

"It was love at first sight for Mary. And he didn't marry her for her looks. It was a plain girl, she was." She stopped, taken aback by her unkind remark and in recompense, hastily added, "It's a good woman Mary is, very devout. She's seen to it that Boylan gave a good bit to the church. She's a homebody and a good mother too, though the two of them were only blessed with but one child, Maureen.

"Anyway, the McCarthys had money; they're financially among the Irish upper crust. Boylan was a calculatin' man, Michael. That's why I favored your uncle. Boylan didn't take me in with all his charm. He's a man that was in the thick of bad things.

"You want to know what Boylan's true love was?"

"You mean he cheated on Mary McCarthy."

Mike's aunt laughed, "Yeah, with his first love-politics. He got on with the Levee Democrats and worked like a beaver for the candidates they put up. Got the voters out. They were grateful. He worked his way up in the party.

"It sounds as if you haven't that much regard for Boylan. So will you be goin' to the wake."

"Who says I've no regard for the man. He was a hustler, but look how he helped your uncle and me," she pointed a finger at Mike, "and you as well after we took you in when your folks died of the typhoid. When he got his saloon with McCarthy as a dowry or whatever, he was even more help to Irish in need. Of course, he was also into boodle and gamblin'. Oh, that the McCarthy's deplored, pious folk that they are. But by then, he wasn't dependent on them no more."

"Aunt Maggie, Karl here is goin' to the wake officially. He's got a rig and needs me, so I'm goin' as well." He turned to Karl. "We can take me Aunt Maggie, too, right?"

"Of course."

"Good, ah Michael, you know I never miss a good wake and this will be a good one. Besides, Mary Boylan deserves a good crowd. She's had to put up with a lot from Patrick Boylan. At least a good sendoff will make her proud. And don't think I've forgotten all that Boylan did for your Uncle Frank and me. No, he was never an ungenerous man. For you too, what with the doctor and sendin' you home in his carriage. There's things I didn't like about Boylan but I will certainly be attendin' his wake. Like I said, he could be a generous man and that's what we should remember about him. My crew of ladies will be handlin' my lunch wagon so I'm concentratin' on the wake. She turned to Weber. "Would you have room in your rig for me and what I need to bring?"

"Yes, I had to rent a big one or get none at all. We'll have plenty of room."

"Good, because I need to be bringin' lots of pies and things. Lots of folks will be comin' out for Boylan's wake. Mary will need every bit of food she can get. She can afford it, mind you, but she won't be up to doin' anything herself right now. Devoted she was to Boylan, and she'll be down now for sure."

"Mrs. Herlihy, I'm thinking that the two of us will be interviewing you some more about Boylan," said Karl.

"When I've the time, I'll be glad to help. Even if Boylan wasn't as saintly as some folks make him out to be," and she looked pointedly at Mike, "he surely didn't deserve to get shot down in cold blood." She shuddered. "And him with all his sins on his soul too." She left the room.

"Mike, did you hear what your aunt said? We'll be needing to hear about those sins."

"Oh, we'll be needin' to check things out but gossip Aunt Maggie hears from women friends and real facts are different things entirely."

"Still wanting to make a hero out of Boylan, are you?"

"Look, the man had his faults, besides you heard Aunt Maggie, he helped folks a lot. Jaysus, he helped me a few weeks ago. Without him I wouldn't be here."

Weber thought Mike's survival owed more to his aunt than to Boylan but decided it was better not to say so. His partner seemed in no mood to have the alderman disparaged. And that puzzled Karl. Mike was always lecturing him about keeping on the straight and narrow. They even called him Father Rafferty at work. Yet here he was defending Boylan, overlooking his corrupt reputation. Then he remembered Rafferty was an orphan. Maybe, thought Karl, Boylan was a father figure to Mike.

While Karl mused, Mike was pouring himself fresh tea, adding more whiskey.

"The big shots won't be coming to the wake until later, and it's their thoughts we'll be wantin' to hear, so we've got a bit of time. In the meantime, I've got more questions. Tell me, have you got the weapon? How many shots did it take to bring him down? Was there a struggle? Was he shot at close range?"

"Boylan was shot twice with a Colt.45," answered Karl, after settling back into the easy chair. "And no, we don't have the weapon. But it was no close up execution, and there was no struggle. He must have been caught by surprise and didn't have time to put up a defense. The fact that the murderer was in the room indicates he wasn't an outright enemy or surely Boylan wouldn't have let him in. Plus he didn't have a gun in hand himself. There was a gun in Boylan's desk, but it hadn't been taken out and it hadn't been used."

"So he thought he had no need for it."

"It seems so. It was two shots in the heart that killed him."

Mike winced.

"And the shots came from halfway across the room."

"I'll be wantin' to see the place for meself. And be talkin' to the barkeeps, that Mrs. Plotz, and those two bodyguards."

"Fitzpatrick and Duffy both appeared to be broken up about the death. A lot of mea culpa and breast beating went on when Steele and I talked to them. A lot of "why wasn't I there when he needed me?" Anticipating Mike's next question, he added, "And it didn't seem like an act to me."

"We need to find out who benefits from the death. I'm not thinkin' about the widow here. I'm meaning who benefits in the Levee. Any word on that?"

"We don't know that yet. We don't know much about his business dealings there at all. Everybody's being evasive or they really don't know. His important papers must be stashed somewhere other than his office. The small safe there had cash and for a man in Boylan's business some mighty innocuous papers." They both sat quietly for a time until Karl broke the silence.

"Listen, maybe you're the one that can answer this question for me. Could this murder have something to do with the Clan na Gael? Could Boylan have been a member on the outs with some of the others in the Clan? Remember what happened to Cronin," he said, referring to a notorious murder case a few years back involving members of the Irish secret society dedicated to subversive activities against England. "Doc Cronin was murdered by those in the Clan he was on the outs with, some of them cops no less."

"You don't have to tell me the particulars. I was on the force then, you weren't. I know the story. I followed the trial." He put up his hands in a gesture of futility. "I'm only a Loyal Hibernian meself. I'm not into secret societies, so I can't tell you for sure if Boylan was a member or not. But even if he was, I never heard that he was actively pursuing that sort of thing. He wasn't on about English crimes in Ireland like some of the others. I think his concerns were for the here and now." Karl looked doubtful so Mike's tone became more vehement. "And just because two cops were involved in the murder, don't think every Irish cop spends his time concocting bomb plots against the English. It's the same with the politicians. Boylan would rant against the Brits at Fourth of July picnics. Shite, that's expected of an Irish politician, but I don't believe it went any further than that."

"But you don't know for sure."

"No, I don't know for sure, but I'm mighty doubtful."

"Mike, aren't Clan members in Chicago involved in local ward politics?"

"Hell yes, even the national chairman of the Clan was involved and after supporting the winner for mayor, he got to appoint friends to the police department."

"And he's the one that got Cronin kicked out of the Clan because he was too moderate."

Grudgingly, Mike admitted as much. "Cronin thought the chairman was too high-handed and said as much, so he got expelled from the Clan. One of Cronin's charges was that Clan funds had been misspent on some forays into Britain. Then when the Brits picked up the bombers right at the dock, the Clan knew that someone had ratted on them."

"I read about that", acknowledged Karl.

"The Clan accused Cronin of being the fellow's pal, and he was called a traitor as well." Mike sighed. "It was all probably trumped up by some of them in the Clan that decided Cronin had to go."

"And then Cronin's mutilated corpse was found in a Lake View catch basin. If it hadn't been for Herman Schuettler--."

"Yeah, a good German cop."

"At least he could be disinterested. He was the one that rooted out Cronin's murderers. Besides you say you're not in the Clan so what are you getting all hot and bothered about?"

"Not being Irish, you wouldn't understand."

"At least consider that Boylan's murder could have something to do with the Clan and sound out sources accordingly. I can't do that. You thought well of the man and you wouldn't want to see the murderer getting away with it, right, Clan member or not?"

"I'll ask around, but this isn't Clan business I tell you, even if Boylan was a member. Don't worry, we're goin' to catch the skunk that did this," Mike declared. He sounded hopeful enough but looked doubtful. Rallying, he emphasized his determination by punching a fist into his open palm but then visibly relaxed. "That's enough of that for now. Tell me what else I've missed being laid up and all."

Relieved the tension had gone out of Mike at least for the moment, Karl said, "We haven't caught our highwayman yet."

"Jaysus, a highwayman in this day and age." Mike snorted derisively, then asked, "Anything new on Bob Scott?"

"Not a thing. Oh, by the way, Martin Burke died at Joliet. He said nothing more about the Cronin case."

"That I didn't know." Then, with a flick of his wrist, he brushed aside the death of one of Cronin's convicted killers. "None of this is as big as the news on Boylan." Karl gave his partner a wary glance but Mike didn't seem inclined to start up again. Instead he just sat back in his chair and quietly drank his tea.

CHAPTER THREE

"Here! It's down this street," Rafferty called out, at the same time rapping on the window dividing him from Karl on the driver's seat, in order to get his attention.

As if I could miss it, thought Karl, as he viewed the phaetons, surreys, broughams, clarences, even a rockaway or two, similar to the rig he'd hired, all converging on the same destination in one of the better neighborhoods in the first ward.

"Quite a proper neighborhood for the Ward," he commented aloud, his breath hanging in the cold air like a cloud, as he observed the statelier brick and stone houses he was passing. "And what a turnout!" Several patrolmen had lanterns lit against the encroaching dusk, directing the unusually heavy traffic by pointing in one direction or another, presumably where parking was to be found.

When one of the patrolmen reached Weber's vehicle, he asked, "Are you folks here for Alderman Boylan's wake?"

"Yes, we are," replied Weber. "And we'd like to get as close as possible for we've food to unload. Besides that-."

"Besides that," added Rafferty, who'd opened his window, "we're here on police business." He was holding up his badge so the uniform could see. The patrolman mulled the information over for a moment, then motioning them forward, walked side-by-side with the

slowly moving rig until he could point down a
side alley.

"Go through there," he said, pointing, "it'll
take you to the rear of Alderman Boylan's house.
They'll make room for you. You'll be able to
park back there as well." The rear of the house,
when they finally reached it, would obviously
have to be shared with a number of other
carriages and wagons. However, as soon as
Weber pulled up, someone appeared from the
carriage house in order to facilitate parking.

"We've food to unload, but we're here for
the wake as well and will be going inside,"
Weber explained to the attendant. The man
immediately directed them to a spot near the back
door.

"Pull up over there. Yes, there, next to the
undertaker's wagon," the man ordered sharply,
impatient at Weber's indecision in moving his
vehicle. "We'll park your rig to a more
convenient spot after you unload. And don't
worry, you'll be able to retrieve it later." Then,
besides helping Mrs. Herlihy to step down, the
man directed flunkies standing about waiting for
instructions to unload the parcels of food and
take them into the kitchen. "You folks just go on
in," he said more courteously, "we'll take care of
your horse and buggy."

A dark wreath with a tasteful purple ribbon
greeted mourners at the back door. Weber and
Rafferty noted it even as they were hustled
forward by someone coming along behind them
with a case of bottles. They found themselves
thrust into a warm and crowded kitchen where

women were dishing out food and directing still more volunteers in its distribution. Mrs. Herlihy recognized friends and immediately began calling out greetings. Some abandoned their tasks to give the newcomer a hug and a kiss. Motioning Rafferty forward, Mrs. Herlihy began the introductions.

"This is me nephew, Michael Rafferty, him what's with the police. Michael, this is Mrs. Liam Sullivan."

Mrs. Sullivan, who'd turned from where she'd been slicing cold meats and was still brandishing a lethal looking knife, exclaimed, "And sure, it's often we've all heard about you from your Aunt Maggie though we've not met until today. And isn't it a downright shame that we had to meet under such awful circumstances." Then noting that Rafferty was taking the slicing knife she was waving around into wary account, she hastily put it down on the counter. She laughed.

"It won't do to be threatening the police with me knife, now will it?" she declared and thrust out her hand to Rafferty. His aunt introduced the other ladies and Rafferty in turn introduced his partner.

"Och, a German detective coming to an Irish wake," exclaimed one of the very oldest ladies present. "Won't he find that a different cup o' tay." She directed her stare to Rafferty. "And will you fellas be investigatin' the untimely death of Alderman Boylan?" Rafferty nodded.

"Good, you just catch the one what done it." Both men assured her they would do just that.

"You know you two missed Carter Harrison. He came early to pay his respects as well he should. The Alderman was his staunch supporter, and I would bet Harrison'll be mayor again." She smiled. "At least so sez me old man."

"I'm impressed," Weber whispered to Rafferty. "I rather favor Harrison myself. I've voted for him in the past."

They were then distracted, for coming into the kitchen in search of more bottles of whiskey was one of Boylan's barmen who recognized Rafferty.

"Oh, it's you Sarge. You fellas go right on into the parlor, the Alderman's laid out there. No need to be hanging around here."

"Are you coming, Aunt Maggie?" asked Rafferty.

"I'll be along as soon as I see that my pies and things are properly unpacked," and she gestured to a spare spot here and a spare spot there so that the fellows still handling her parcels could stow them safely.

"The Missus will be that pleased with your contribution, Maggie," offered Mrs. Sullivan, "for we've quite a crowd already and more folks are sure to come. For sure, the Alderman was a popular man. And you fellas," she added, turning her attention to the two detectives, "before you go on into the parlor, leave your coats and things upstairs. Missus Boylan's maids are taking care of all that." Rafferty motioned Weber to follow, and they headed for the rooms at the front of the house. This necessitated stepping past men coming and going or simply standing around discussing this or that but mostly, and in subdued whispers, exchanging information about the murder. Liquor was already being served and many of the men held glasses in one hand and a cigar or cigarette in the other.

"Boylan will be in the front parlor," said Rafferty softly. "Let's get rid of our coats and then pay our respects. After that, we can look around and see who else is attendin'." Karl nodded even as he began unwinding his scarf and removing his mittens and hat. After coming back downstairs, both men noted it was a large house and all the downstairs rooms and halls had been given over to those who'd come to pay their last respects. In the large front parlor, which had been lengthened by opening the sliding doors between it and the dining room, all the plush furniture normally present had been removed and replaced by chairs. These were largely occupied by women, the men circulating freely elsewhere or lining the walls of the rooms. At one end of the parlor under a large crucifix and near a bay window with closed dark velvet drapes was a raised gray and silver casket heaped about with floral sprays and wreaths, so many, that the room was heavy with their scent.

"That's the Missus and the daughter," said Rafferty, indicating two females sitting in the front row surrounded by sobbing women heavily encased in shawls and rocking back and forth in the accepted manner of official mourners.

As they stepped into the room, a man appeared out of one of the dark corners and confronted them. He had such a lugubrious expression on his face, that Rafferty took him to be one of the undertaker's assistants. He was correct in his assessment because the man immediately asked them, in a soft whisper, if they wished to pay their respects. Receiving an affirmative reply, he escorted them to the front of the room before returning to his assigned post. At the casket, several priests hovered adding their bit of piety, to the scene. The two detectives recognized some of their plainclothes colleagues as well as a number of precinct captains in uniform-all of them flanking the wall between paintings of pastoral scenes. They received recognition in return, exchanging mutual nods and gestures.

Rafferty nudged his partner and indicated Kevin Fitzpatrick and Brian Duffy standing at sentinel attention, one on either side of the coffin. Duffy, Rafferty was glad to see, had left off his more flamboyant clothes and was clad in more appropriate somber black. Fitzpatrick was in the same conservative dark suit he'd sported in Boylan's saloon and except for the difference between a suit and a cassock could still, in Rafferty's opinion, have passed for one of the clergy.

"A lot of good those two fellows are now," he whispered discreetly in an aside to Weber before adding, "We'd best go up and pay our respects." He strode to the front of the room until he reached the casket, Weber right behind him. lowering themselves onto the red velvet kneeler provided, they both examined the deceased.

Boylan's head was resting on a white silk pillow and a rosary was draped through his fingers.

The undertaker's done a good job, thought Rafferty. Boylan looks downright peaceful. He still looked the big man he'd been in life and filled the coffin. He didn't need the soft flattering light of the candles and lowered gaslight to look handsome. Rafferty hadn't seen many better looking corpses including his Uncle Frank. He remembered the last time he'd seen Boylan and his eyes grew moist. Reaching quickly for a handkerchief, he wiped away the threatening tears and swore under his breath, vowing to catch him that did the murder.

The two sergeants rose in unison and turned to the widow. Rafferty's aunt had entered the parlor and was bent over Mrs. Boylan offering condolences. The widow, a short heavy set women clad all in black, called over to Duffy and asked him to get an extra chair for her friend. Before he returned from his errand, Mrs. Herlihy introduced her nephew and his partner.

"Patrick mentioned you to me many times, Sergeant Rafferty," said the widow, who had a face a bit like some of his aunt's unbaked dough making him immediately recall his aunt's unflattering comments on Mary Boylan's looks. On the other hand, he couldn't appraise the daughter at all since the upper half of her body was completely shrouded by a long black veil. "The Alderman took an interest in your career. He was always helping others. He was a good man, wasn't he?"

"He was that, Ma'am. I admired him a lot."

"He looks lovely, doesn't he?" she asked, nodding toward the casket. Rafferty agreed that Boylan did indeed look his best. "Even the Archbishop came to pay his respects," the widow continued. "John was always a friend of the church. He was a good man, wasn't he?" she asked again, but in a definite manner, then pausing, as if waiting for affirmation. The women in her immediate vicinity hastened to agree, saying that yes, indeed, Alderman Boylan was a good man. Before the widow could nod in satisfaction an older man seated directly behind her emitted a snort of derision.

Mike looked at the lone dissenter with some interest. Flanking the old man on either side were two younger men who bore a striking resemblance to the widow, they all appeared baked from the same dough. Mrs. Boylan heard the snort but gave no more indication than a slight frown. The two younger men had immediately bent toward the older fellow and urgently shushed him.

Making way for someone else wanting to offer their condolences, Rafferty motioned Weber to the back of the room. A man was trying to enter with a glass in his hand but the glares of the women and hissing sounds and shooing motions from the undertaker's assistant caused his ignominious retreat.

Mike waited until that dour gentleman had finished his attentions to the drunk, then asked, "Who are those fellas sittin' right behind Mrs. Boylan.

"Why, that's Mr. McCarthy, Mrs. Boylan's father, and the two men on either side of him are her brothers."

Mike motioned Karl away from the parlor. "Looks like old McCarthy didn't much approve of his son-in-law," he said. "Maybe we should be askin' him and his boys a few questions."

"You can't make a murder motive out of a snort of disapproval. But you're right, talking to them might be revealing."

"So we'll add them to the list." Mike looked around at the crowds. "Let's see what's going on in the other rooms. Folks can't talk too freely here," he said indicating their proximity to the parlor and its bier. They went on into still another room where the Alderman's own barkeeps were pouring out drinks and where generous servings of food were also set out.

Rafferty had noticed Weber's earlier surprise at the keening women and now took note of his additional surprise at the steady flow of liquor. "You Germans don't know how to give a fellow a good send-off."

"Of course we do. We lay out a spread after the funeral for those who've taken the trouble to come, and we have wakes for the deceased. But they're not like this." He waved in the direction of the small clusters of men. "And from what I can hear, it's beginning to sound like a political rally. It's excessive, I think."

"We're celebrating the deceased, may God bless Patrick Boylan," retorted Rafferty. "Boylan turned out for lots of others including me Uncle Frank. He helped with their spreads if help was needed and so he deserves a good show himself. Besides, wakes are for the living. The widow will see that her man was loved and highly regarded."

Already provided with his own glass of good Irish whiskey, Weber shrugged rather than continue the discussion and both men began surveying the room to see who else was in attendance. There were plenty of blue uniforms. Boylan knew a lot of policemen, thought Rafferty. Boylan paid off a lot of policemen, thought Weber. A lot of cassocks were in attendance as well because Boylan had been a great financial supporter of the church, and the clergy obviously savored a glass of good whiskey as well as the next man. Rafferty recognized Knobby and some of his cronies stuffing themselves with final handouts from their chief.

"That's one of Boylan's electoral helpers over there, the one with the lumpy head."

"He looks like he's been knocked around a good bit."

"He's the one that does the knockin'. He gets out the votes."

"Like that, is it?" Weber smiled. Rafferty nodded.

"There's plenty of ward bosses here and plenty of city employees, and they're not putting in an appearance just because they've been pressured to show up. Boylan was a popular man." He moved into the hallway and looked into the other rooms. One, now full of men smoking and drinking, seemed to have served as a study or an office for the alderman. A large and impressive mahogany desk was at one end of the room also cabinets with multiple drawers. In addition the walls were well lined with books.

"Looks like Boylan was a reader," commented Weber. He gave the books a closer inspection and shook his head. "It's a library bought whole for decoration. Nothing looks read." He pulled out a few of the volumes, then returned them to the shelves.

"Untouched as far as I can see. Some of the pages aren't even cut." He gestured toward the desk. "We haven't had a chance to go through his papers here yet and that has to be done. Like I told you, Steele went through the papers in his private office at the saloon, but they weren't much. A better cache of papers has got to be here somewhere. Maybe they're in that desk or in those cabinets." It was obvious from the way Weber was moving around, he was itching to start looking then and there.

"Look at everyone standing around. Stuff could easily get taken. Maybe it's gone already," he fretted.

"Which we can't do anything about right now but what we could and should be doin' is listenin' and maybe askin' a thing or two of some of these folks here," said Rafferty dismissing Weber's anxieties. He was interrupted by a commotion out in the hall and both detectives stepped to the doorway to see what had caused the ruckus. There were murmurs of "tis Bathhouse John hisself". And it was Bathhouse John Coughlin, surrounded by a cortege of his own, making a grand entrance. The man couldn't help stirring up a crowd. Six foot tall with a thick bull neck and powerful through the shoulders and chest, Bathhouse John also sported a full mustache and long sideburns. Having a penchant for flamboyance in dress added considerably to his visibility, even though it had been toned down in respect for the deceased. But even in black, there was something flashy about Coughlin. His black was shinier, his diamond stick pin had more glitter, his gold watch and chain were bigger and heavier and had to cover an even greater expanse of stomach than most folks could boast.

"I expect if Coughlin's here, Mike Kenna will be coming too," said Weber.

"Not necessarily, the Dink doesn't like wakes or funerals. It's only a rare one he'll attend. So he might not grace this one either, though he'll send the usual flowers and condolences, and in this case have masses read. And as important as Kenna is, he can't count on that to turn folks out when his own time comes. If you don't go to wakes and funerals, friends and relations of all those you've ignored won't bother coming to yours." Weber smiled at Rafferty's bit of wisdom regarding funeral customs.

"Where's me old pal?" Coughlin called loudly. "Where's Paddy Boylan? I've come to pay me respects to the grand fella." His adherents carved a path to the bier for him, and the two detectives discreetly followed the procession. At the casket, Coughlin knelt by himself and said his prayers. He produced a large handkerchief and gave a loud honk before turning to the widow and paying his condolences. "Any help you need,

Mary Boylan, you can count on me," he declared while patting her hand. "Everyone knows how devoted John was to his family, to his community, and to the church. His friends could always depend on him as could the poor."

At each compliment, the widow nodded. There were murmurs of approval from around the room which Coughlin acknowledged with a slight nod until the widow said thank you and dismissed him. With a final bow in her direction, he turned, at the same time issuing greetings to a pal here and an acquaintance there besides managing to nod his head piously in the direction of the priestly contingent. Then, in a sort of triumphal parade, he made his way to where food and drink were being served. Weber, obviously fascinated by Coughlin, watched closely as the big man fortified with a glass of whiskey, wiped away a tear and began pontificating on the deceased.

"A tragic end it was for me old pal. Devout he was, a good friend to the church, a good family man. Good to his friends, good to the poor and needy, good for Chicago, and a good Democrat all his life. You can rest assured that I'll be doing me best to get this murder solved. I'll be after them detectives. I'll be telling the police to be getting down to the business of catching the blackguard that done the dirty deed." He paused and the crowd surged around him eagerly agreeing with everything he said.

"Have we just heard some vote-getting sentiments?" asked Weber.

"Of course we have. Politikin' and wakes go hand in hand even when the deceased's a lowly sewer worker or owns just a bit of a business, so even the poorest soul usually gets a good turnout," explained Rafferty, though he looked a bit put out. "But I can't say I like Bathhouse John stealin' Boylan's thunder." A second thought made him shrug. "At least with Boylan, the eulogies are true. When the politicos praise some of them other dead fellows, only a mother would make a connection between the eulogy and the deceased."

Someone came to stand in front of them. It was Kevin Fitzpatrick.

"Are you going to be on the case, Sergeant Rafferty?"

"I expect I will, along with Sergeant Weber here. And we'll be talkin' to you."

Fitzpatrick nodded. "Me and Brian Duffy want to help in any way we can." The corners of his mouth turned down. "Him and me, we loved Alderman Boylan. He was good to us, so we'll be ready and waiting for anything you've got to ask." He hesitated, then shaking himself, he muttered, "Sorry, duty calls." But far from going back to the role of sentinel at the casket, he retreated glass in hand to the table where food was set out and where Bathhouse John was having a plate heaped for himself.

"I wonder if he's going to attach himself to Coughlin now?"

"To him or to some other boss," said Rafferty in a sad voice. Whispers began again out in the hallway indicating Johnny Powell had arrived. "Johnny DePow, sachem of the Nineteenth, explained Rafferty. "Now he never misses a wake or a burial. There's no love lost between Powell and Coughlin, but I expect out of respect for Boylan, they'll not be crossin' swords today. They'll both be doin' some politikin' though from opposite ends of the room."

"Michael Rafferty, is that you? I thought you was at death's door." A tall cadaverous man, looking as if he'd undergone a graver illness than Rafferty, squinted at them both through narrow suspicious eyes.

"Luckily, I didn't have to step inside," retorted Rafferty. "And for that I can thank Boylan, his whiskey, his kindness in lending me a rig the night the illness come over me, and his own doctor to boot."

The man's head went up and down slowly in an attempt at a sage response.

"It's good to see you back in fightin' form."

"This here's me partner, Karl Weber. Karl, this is Sergeant Aloyius Ryan out of the Nineteenth. Probably came with Johnny DePow." Again the man nodded.

"I hear you downtown fellas have the case. Got any leads? No?" he said when they didn't reply. " Me, I think you'll have a tough time of it. Boylan was into too many things. The murder could have been the result of any of them."

Mike frowned at Ryan.

"We'll be checkin' on all of 'em. But if there's something you know you'd best be tellin' us."

Ryan shook his head.

"Nah, I just know he was into this and that."
Mike looked at him as if he expected more
information, so he continued. "Everybody knows
about the gamblin' and the open saloons and his
deals with some of the other politicos and the big
money men. Those fellas may live refined lives,"
and he made a point of drinking a pretend cup of
something with his pinky extended, "but they can
play rough. And Boylan, he had some houses
too."

"What do you mean he had some houses?"
demanded Mike.

"Check it out. Rumor has it that he was into
prostitution in a big way in spite of his pious
posing."

"Listen, Ryan, I never heard anything about
that, and furthermore, I don't believe a word of
it."

Ryan shrugged. It was all one to him. He
wasn't on the case. Boylan hadn't been any pal of
his. He was a Powell man. He saluted Rafferty
and turned to the food and whiskey.

Mike sneered at Ryan's back.

"Hope the Hull House ladies give Powell a
run for his money. It would fix Ryan's wagon all
right if an honest man finally got elected in the
Nineteenth."

"What are you talking about?"

"Jane Addams and her Hull House crew
think Johnny Powell's an evil influence on her
poor immigrants, and she's itching to run
someone against him. More power to her says I."
He sighed, "Though she ain't really got a
chance."

"A lot of Levee bigwigs are into prostitution, Mike," said Weber, changing the subject back to Ryan's suggestion. "Boylan could have been as well." Mike shook his head. His expression was so mulish, Weber went no further but he thought it might be worthwhile talking to Aloyius Ryan again sometime. He knew as they continued investigating that if anything of what Ryan hinted at was going on, it was bound to come out. But better sooner than later. Hell, the Levee made Sodom and Gomorrah look good and Boylan was bound to be involved. *Still, why should I aggravate Mike now? Let him find out for himself if it's true about Boylan.*

As far as Weber was concerned all the Levee politicians were tainted and had their hands in the worst sort of rackets. The newspapers all agreed and drummed it into the ears of Chicago readers day after day. It's what he heard over the dinner table from his father and brother when he went home for visits.

His father was in the newspaper business and though it was only a German daily, he heard some of the same things the *Tribune* and *Globe* reporters did and passed them on to his son. And kept passing them on, so his son would know the dirty business he was in, leave the police, and go into a more honorable profession. Dealing with crime was close to heresy in the Weber family, even though Karl was supposedly on the side of right.

Karl's thoughts went back to Rafferty. He knew that if Mike did find out anything derogatory about his hero, he wouldn't cover up.

He was far too honest for that. Karl smiled to himself. *He's got one hell of a conscience riding him.* His own he knew was a trifle more flexible.

Weber looked around, "Say, Mike, quite a few attractive young ladies seem to be here, and young men as well. Could they all be friends of Maureen McCarthy?"

"Nah, a wake is a respectable place to be sizing up potential mates. You know, to meet the opposite sex in respectable surroundings. Find out the names, et cetera."

"I never thought of a wake as a matrimonial bureau." And both men laughed.

Someone came up to them declaring it was a grand wake.

"I been to a good many wakes in me time, fellas, but this is one of the grandest. What a spread! What a spread, eh fellas? Thank God for good old Boylan." None too steadily the man moved on to others in the crowd, each time declaring his pleasure over and over again. The murder seemed to have been set aside in people's minds. Some of the talk around the two detectives was eulogizing, but most of it was plain politics, especially speculation about who would take Boylan's place on the City Council. Speculation said that Coughlin was in the lead. Other names were mentioned, all of them duly noted by Weber and Rafferty, as their various chances to gain the seat were assessed. Then Coughlin could be heard sending someone out for boxes of cigars to pass around before turning back to talk still more politics.

"It's politics and more politics here tonight. I wish they'd speculate on the murder."

"What can you expect, Karl? These men are all heavily involved in city affairs, and they're considering what concerns them most. If they were all churchmen, I expect, they'd be discussing religion. When the time comes and the priest calls us to order, we'll all be bending the knee praying for Boylan and forget the politics for a bit."

"By all accounts, he'll be needing all the prayers he can get," said a voice behind them.

"Jaysus, Maxwell, how'd you get in?"

"Rafferty, this is news, and I go where there's news."

"Where there's food by the looks of it as well," said Weber with a grin, eyeing both the heaping plate the Globe reporter was carrying and his well-stocked figure.

"Anything new on the murder?" Maxwell lowered his voice which continued to be amiable in spite of Weber's sarcastic remark.

"The news, when there is any, will be coming from headquarters not from the likes of us," replied Rafferty.

"You two probably don't know anything." Maxwell forked up some ham and chewed and swallowed before hinting. "You might want to talk to me. We reporters hear things, you know. I could tell you a few interesting things about Boylan."

"Ahh, and just what is it you dish up? Rumors or facts," sneered Rafferty.

"Rumors. It's up to you two to prove that they're facts." Maxwell gave them a big smile before looking around the room. "Quite a crowd. Maybe Mayor Washburne, will be along and I hear Lattimore's coming too. A lone Republican in this den of Democrats. I don't feel a bit sorry for him though. He's a shark like the rest of them and can take care of himself." Maxwell looked at them. "Ain't you fellows eating? I mean this is an outstanding spread." They said nothing and with a wave he departed seeking further sustenance.

"We should talk to him, Mike. Reporters hear stuff. They have sources."

"Yeah, of unsubstantiated dirt."

"Listen, we've worked with Maxwell before, and you know he isn't that bad."

"I got to admit he ain't the worst. You're right; we'll talk to him. Set something up." He paused considering their agenda. "We'll have to go to the funeral too. It's the day after tomorrow. Even in this cold, Boylan won't keep forever. Let's go in a rig. It's police business and the city can pay. Besides, there's only so much public transport I'm ready to subject meself to yet. Agreed?"

He waved away the cigar smoke beginning to make visibility difficult and which long since had triumphed over any lingering floral scent. Karl agreed, and they scrutinized the men coming and going. It was pitch dark outside and still folks were coming to pay their last respects, the poorer sort of folks, mostly men, coming caps in hand after work to pay homage to the man who had helped them out with a load of coal or maybe a job or at least an annual turkey at Christmas, and for whom they'd voted in election after election--sometimes more than once. But the politicians weren't removing themselves, as there was still plenty to discuss and strategy to plan, as well as a public face to be shown. Rafferty and Weber could hear some of the newcomers commenting on the bosses around them.

"Ah, ain't that just like Bathhouse," said one such fellow as he was handed a cigar by one of Coughlin's men. The donor nodded in the direction of Bathhouse John so there'd be no mistake about the source of the cigar. The recipient acknowledged the donation by a bow in Coughlin's direction and the big man nodded affably back. "Yes, he's always there when a fella needs help, just like old Boylan, may God rest his soul and damn his murderer to hell." Waving Coughlin's cigars, the man's cronies all agreed with the sentiment. Then they heaved a collective sigh.

"What are we goin' to do for jobs now that Boylan's gone."

"You'll see. Bathhouse and the Dink will take up the slack. God, I hope he's a good one like old Boylan."

Another man waving his gift cigar reminded them of still another wake.

"Remember when Joe Flynn fell down his cellar stairs going to get a bucket of coal. Yes, him that was a cousin of the Head of the Sewer Department. He broke his neck, poor auld Flynn, but his cousin gave him a grand turnout."

"You're right. It wasn't as good as this though."

"Well, there's no comparison between Boylan and Joe Flynn. But it was a pretty good wake for a fella that worked in the sewers."

"That I'll admit."

There was a sudden silence. All talk ceased. Glasses raised to lips stopped. All eyes turned to the doorway, there were a few sharp intakes of breath. Then a man stepped forward. Mike glanced at Coughlin, and for once, even Bathhouse John was speechless. In fact, he looked downright floored.

"Mr. Coughlin," said the newcomer, advancing on Bathhouse John.

"Mr. Yerkes, " replied Coughlin, recovering his aplomb and striding forward, a hand as big as a frying pan extended in welcome.

Whispers passed rapidly around the room. "Jaysus, tis Mr. Yerkes hisself come to see off our Paddy."

"Well, well," said Karl softly to Mike, "the most notorious robber baron in Chicago."

"Yeah, him that half the street car strap-hangers would dearly love to see swinging from a lamppost. He makes Purcell, the old traction king, look good."

"He probably had plenty of shady deals going with Boylan."

Mike let the remark pass, he was too busy examining the man Chicago newspapers loved to lampoon for his methods. Bathhouse John himself was leading Yerkes to the main parlor for a viewing.

"This won't break up until the rosary is said," murmured Mike suddenly looking tired.

"I'll take you and your aunt home afterwards, of course," said Weber, belatedly realizing what a strain the occasion must be for his recently recovered partner.

"Listen, stay over," suggested Mike. "We've got a spare bedroom. Then you and I can drive to City Hall in relative comfort tomorrow morning. Anyway you don't want to be drivin' all the way to our house then back to some livery stable downtown, and then travel clear to the north side to your own place. Shite, the way the streets are in some places, you and that rig could fall into some hole in the dark, and we'd never hear from you again."

Mulling over the suggestion only briefly, Weber agreed it was a good plan. Eyeing his taller partner, Mike cracked a smile, "I'll even loan you one of me nightshirts, though it's bound to be a mite short." They both smiled. Karl nodded to the food. They dished up hearty platefuls and went back to surveying and listening to the crowd.

CHAPTER FOUR

Mike stood in the entrance taking in all of
the folks assembled in the lobby of City Hall.
"Jaysus," he exclaimed, before venturing inside,
"It's the same as ever. Every ward heeler in
Chicago, everyone lookin' for a handout from the
politicos and, of course, the reporters, you can't
keep them away either." He looked around. "I see
the uniforms haven't rousted out all the bums."

"It's that time of year again, Mike," said
Karl, who was standing right behind him. "You
know they let the homeless in out of the cold
after hours."

"I know, I know, and what poor sod
wouldn't rather sleep on marble floors than doss
down in the local lock-up. I just hope any fleas
on 'em settle on the ward heelers." He began
forcing his way with a prod here and a nudge
there through the smokers whose countless
cigars, cigarettes, and pipes emitted a dense layer
of smoke. A few of the men in the lobby

recognized the two detectives and tossed out brief greetings.

One reporter sidled up, asking, "Hey, Rafferty, Weber, are you two working the Boylan case? How about a tidbit or two?"

"We ain't got a thing for you," groused Mike. Karl agreed with a shrug signifying "sorry," and the disappointed reporter returned his pencil and notebook to his pocket before turning back to a political discussion he'd abandoned. The various arguments and conversations swirling around the two detectives contributed as much to the hot air in the lobby as the hissing steam radiators did.

At the stairs, Mike was welcomed back by the uniformed cops on duty.

"Rafferty, it's good to see ya back."

"Mike, glad you made it."

"Hey, we was worried about ya, Rafferty."

"Looks like you're popular, Mike," said Karl to his grinning colleague.

"It's gratifying to know that fellow humans think I make the grade."

"Ah, no," called Officer Mulcahy, "it's me old pal, Rafferty, come back to us. I heard tell that you was at Death's door. But thanks be to God, he decided against lettin' ya in." He looked Mike over more critically and tsked in disapproval.. "Ye've lost weight, lad, and ya can't afford it. Ya got to put it back on. Some of that good German cooking should do the trick. Weber, you've got to steer him to the right places."

"I'll try my best," Karl laughed.

Leaving Officer Mulcahy behind, Mike commented, "How he could tell I've lost weight, bundled up as I am against the cold, is beyond me. But then he's always considered me a runt because I don't bust the buttons off me coat like he does." He looked over at Weber. "I don't need a nursemaid," he added so testily that Karl put his hands up in a gesture of self-defense. "As it is, I got an aunt that treats me like some snot-nosed little kid," he grumbled, at the same time tugging ineffectively at the scarf she'd wrapped multiple times around his neck.

In the detective bureau, while the two men stood removing their coats, Mike replied to more greetings and good wishes from his colleagues. Hearing the noise, Lieutenant Steele stepped out of his office, added a brief welcome of his own, then promptly shifted the two men into the small room, shutting the door behind them. "You two sure showed up late," he said impatiently. "It's almost one o'clock."

"It's a long drive from the west side, Lieutenant. We also attended the funeral mass this morning, then I had to return the rig I rented."

"I should have gone to the service myself, so I guess I can't complain. How useful was it to attend?"

"Not very. We saw almost the same folks as we did last night at the wake."

"So the two of you did get to Boylan's wake yesterday?" Karl nodded. "Any results from that visit?"

"A few more possibilities we can add to list of suspects. Plus a few more leads to follow up," replied Karl for the two of them.

"Don't be forgettin' Yerkes' visit to the wake. I wonder what the likes of him was doin' there. Ah, probably just acknowledgin' his fellow boodlers."

"Well, Lieutenant, it seems there was no love lost between Boylan and his in-laws." Steele looked skeptical at this bit of information.

"What made you draw that conclusion?"

"We saw for ourselves the attitude of old McCarthy to his son-in-law, and we asked a few folks how they got along with the deceased. It seems the family didn't like the way Boylan carried on, you know, with the gambling and the boodle. And he pretty much ignored his wife as well. Their attitude seemed to be good riddance. They've been bad-mouthing Boylan for years. He seemed promising before the marriage. He's, that is, *was*, a well set up man. It was their money that set him up in the saloon business and that they could have stomached, but not the other stuff. They're in with the church, you see. "

Heck, the brothers had public arguments with him. No one mentioned any physical assaults though."

"Sounds weak to me but then I don't know them. Follow it up if you think it's worthwhile. What else?"

"Maxwell of the Globe hinted that he might be able to help." Steele winced; he took a dim view of reporters. For him they meant nothing but mischief and just got in the way during an investigation. "Officer Ryan, who came with the Powell party, told us that Boylan kept whorehouses." Rafferty snorted, but Weber continued in spite of his partner's overt skepticism. "That's a cutthroat business and it's an angle worth exploring. Boylan must have been into shadier businesses than just gambling in the First Ward and payoffs at City Hall. He must have made lots of enemies."

Steele gave them a rueful look.

"Maybe the man got his just deserts, but he was popular all the same and the pressure's on to solve this one. Even Yerkes is singing the man's praises and demanding action."

"Yeah, he was there at the wake," admitted Mike.

"The Gold Coast rubbing noses with First Ward grafters. I should have been there to see that. Still, Yerkes is as much of a miscreant as they are. It's just that he calls it business. It's more respectable when he does it."

"Yerkes is getting to be too much for businessmen like Marshall Field," contributed Karl. "I think they'd like to stop dealing with him. He makes no bones about being a robber baron. He's too obvious for them. He gives them all a black eye."

"Let's get back to Boylan," interrupted Mike. "I want to hear for myself what Duffy, Fitzpatrick, and his barkeeps have to say. The Plotz woman too. I'm not saying you didn't do your job, Karl, but I might be able to get a different slant on things. After all, I knew the man better than you two."

"I wonder if you really did know him, Mike," suggested Karl. Mike brushed the comment aside with a wave of the hand and waited for Steele's answer.

After thinking the matter over for a few moments, the Lieutenant said, "Go to it then. You and Karl do the interviews again. If anyone would know about the man's interest in whorehouses, those flunkies of his would. And for God's sake try to find out where the man's books are, his real business records."

"What did you find in his safe, Lieutenant?" asked Mike.

"Money he used to cash paychecks and a reasonable amount for operating expenses, plus monies he was holding for this, that, and the other fellow, all duly marked. You know, for the small fellow that didn't have a safe of his own."

"That's common practice for saloon owners," observed Karl.

"There was also a set of books that made his whole operation look on the up and up, yet we know the man had gambling rooms. Hell, they should have been raided and closed, but the local precinct never did a damn thing. He was operating his place past regulated hours and got away with that too. He sure greased all the right palms. I've checked and whenever there was a raid, he was as clean as a whistle. He must have got tip-offs when the police were coming."

Rafferty looked annoyed; the lieutenant looked exasperated.

"Mike, go and look at the papers on your desk. There's a few that need signing." Mike nodded but he got up reluctantly. Meanwhile Steele motioned Weber to stay.

Once the door was closed, Steele continued, "Karl, if there's dirt to be found, find it. It will give us a better handle on his enemies. Mike's being unrealistic about Boylan." He tugged at one side of his mustache and that seemed to help him come to a decision. "I'll let him do the interviews again. That's needed in any case. See if you can find the men who ran his gambling rooms. We weren't able to get hold of them since everyone was denying that gambling was actually going on. Maybe, Mike can get to them. I couldn't."

He paused to give the matter more thought and then remarked, "I'm not really worried about Mike. I think he's too honest to cover up if he finds out something about Boylan that brings down his hero a peg. He's determined to catch the murderer and that's what we all want. Just keep a bit of an eye on him, eh, Karl."

Mike glowered at his partner as he approached. "The lieutenant told you to keep an eye on me, didn't he? Well, I don't need a nursemaid on this either."

Karl didn't deny Mike's accusation but added, "You need a partner and that's what I am. We're working together on this, so don't get your temper up."

Rafferty slowly calmed.

"Ah, what the hell," he finally declared.

"Anyway, it's past our lunch hour. Let's grab a bite to eat. We can hop a cable car to Boylan's and eat somewhere close by.

Afterwards, we'll start our interviews with the bartenders at his place and with Mrs. Plotz. And I know you want to see the scene of the crime. Oh, and Steele hopes you can get the names of the gambling room employees. Steele ran into a brick wall there."

Following Weber's plan they reached Boylan's place after a quick lunch, Mike blocking off Karl's further efforts to secure more substantial fare eaten at a more leisurely pace.

The expressions when the bartenders saw the detectives were ones of both wariness and weariness. Sloan answered for all of them when he said, "Not again. We been interviewed by the uniforms, by you fellas from City Hall, by the damned reporters, even Bathhouse John came and gave it a try. Thought he'd start his own investigation. Even the Dink got in a few licks." He looked pointedly at Karl. "Don't you fellas take notes?"

"There's a new man on the block now," retorted Karl, "and he wants to hear it too. The barkeep looked at Rafferty with a disapproving eye, then shrugging in resignation, he indicated a corner table with his thumb. A member of the cleanup crew hastened to wipe it down.

"Yeah, I know you. Rafferty, right?" Mike nodded. "You was pals with Boylan. You can start with me," announced Sloan, seating himself in a relaxed and insolent manner. Mike took him through the discovery of the body and the events of the evening before the murder, but Sloan

didn't add anything to what he'd said in his
earlier interview with Karl and the Lieutenant.
"Sure, Boylan, had enemies," declared Sloan.
"He wasn't in the grocery business. But I can't
give you any specific names. I've talked it over
with the others," he said, nodding toward the bar,
"even with the janitors what clean the place.
We've done our own speculatin', and there's just
no one we can think of who could have done the
deed."

"How many years have you been with
Boylan?" asked Mike.

"A pretty long while, ever since he opened
this place. The Alderman paid better'n the other
saloon owners, and we could eat for free. He
didn't watch every nickel like some of them other
owners. Some stand over the till watchin' a fella
every minute. Hell, chefs get fifty to eighty
dollars a month. I even know janitors pulling in
seventy-five. We put in the same long hours, I
can tell you, and at least Boylan did better than
the twenty-five a month some of those
cheapskates pay their bartending crews.

"What about the card sharps upstairs?" asked
Karl after Sloan wound down from his polemic.

Sloan's eyes grew wide and innocent.

"What card sharps? Ain't no gamblin' goin'
on here. You can see that for yourselves."

"Who's running the place now?" asked
Weber, exasperated with Sloan, who was
grinning at him slyly.

"The widow sent one of her beefy brothers."
He snorted in derision. "Mr. James J. McCarthy.
Hah, Jimmy the Butcher. He don't know beans

about this business. The place's already going downhill. If Missus Boylan's smart, she'll sell soon. If she lets that ignoramus run it, it'll just lose money, and the value of the place'll go down. I'm goin' to look for a new spot meself. Experienced bartenders can always get a job in this town. Chicago's got more bars per square mile than any other city in this country." He leaned closer to Karl. "Or maybe I'll apply at one of those nice quiet German beer gardens. That'd be restful, eh, Sergeant Weber?" He sat back again, this time tucking his thumbs under his suspenders and looking self-satisfied.

"I been savin' my pennies and maybe I'll get a place of my own. I know all about dealin' with the breweries and the liquor interests, and they'll set a man up."

Rafferty leaned closer to Sloan. "We need to talk to Boylan's employees on the other side. You know them and where they're holed up now. We don't care that they ran the gambling rooms. What we want to know is what they saw and what they think about Boylan's murder. No one's goin' to report them or turn them in. You've got my word for that."

He let Sloan stew about that for a few minutes and the man finally nodded.

"Give us their location." He presented Sloan with a pencil and paper. Still, though somewhat reluctantly, he did give them an address.

"If you talk to the one, he can tell you where the others have skedaddled. Tell him, that if I trust you enough to hand over his address, he can trust you as well. I also wrote that you was pals with Boylan."

Just then one of the barkeeps came over. "Hey, Sloan, the brewery dray's here with the order."

Sloan rose at once.

"Mr. James J. McCarthy ought to be dealing with this stuff."

Mike put up a hand to stop him. "Before you go, tell me who dealt with the liquor interests."

"Boylan, of course."

"Sure'n he must have been too busy for that."

"Listen, he did a lot of that himself. Oh, maybe, now and then he'd use Fitzpatrick or Duffy or me, but he liked to be talking to those fellas. He liked to shoot the breeze with all kinds of different folks." Sloan was obviously itching to get away, so Mike demanded to know where Mrs. Plotz was.

"In the kitchen like always. Someone's got to keep the free lunch comin'."

"Take us there then," ordered Rafferty. Sloan grimaced, told the barman that had summoned him he'd only be a minute, and motioned the detectives to follow as he headed for the backrooms of the saloon. On the way, Mike insisted on looking at the layout and to this end entered the various back rooms while Sloan fretted. One room must have been used for large private parties as the two detectives could see tables, chairs, even a piano on a dais. Another room was used for storing kegs and bottles of every sort. Mike even paused to look into a room to the side holding mops, buckets, and brooms. Then at the rear of the saloon complex, guaranteeing that any hot food coming to the bar would be lukewarm, was the kitchen where Mrs. Plotz was busy stirring something in a pot.

"Here's the police again, Plotzie, come to ask more questions." Sloan left with a smirk on his face after filching some sausage and a roll.

"That one, he has no respect for a poor old lady." She turned and looked belligerently at the two detectives from behind her short stub of a nose. "And you don't neither or you wouldn't be bothering Mrs. Plotz again. She's already answered all the questions this fella asked." She pointed at Weber with her cooking spoon and in the process deposited sauce on his coat.

"We need to be asking again," replied Karl in an aggrieved tone of voice as he hastily wiped his coat with a handkerchief. "Maybe you've remembered something since we spoke the last time."

"Mrs. Plotz has said all she is going to say. She knows nothing. She's just a poor widow. And what's going to happen to Mrs. Plotz now, I ask you?" Having set aside her cooking spoon, she stood short, stout, and fierce, with arms akimbo and angrily eyeing the two men. "Mrs. Plotz, she didn't murder nobody," she loudly declared. She so determinedly referred to herself as if she were another person that both detectives were tempted to look into the corners of the kitchen to see if the real Mrs. Plotz might be lurking there.

"Mr. Boylan," she continued, "he was Mrs. Plotz's friend. When Mr. Plotz, who worked for the city in garbage, was killed by a train at one of them damned crossings, it was Mr. Boylan who helped out. He gave the poor widow a job. Did the railroad pay anything? Not a dime. Them trains are killing and crippling folks all the time and do the big shots that run the railroad care? I read the papers; it's one a day and at least two or three injured. No sir, they do not care!"

Weber interrupted in order get back to the business of the murder.

"Mrs. Plotz, we want to hear again if anything unusual happened the night before the murder. In fact, go over the events for us again... and in detail."

But Mrs. Plotz had her own agenda. "What's going to happen to Mrs. Plotz now that Mister Boylan's gone? Mr. Boylan gave Mrs. Plotz a place to stay. But this brother-in-law of his, this McCarthy, this butcher, he don't know nothing about running a saloon. Soon there won't be a business. Then what will happen to Mrs. Plotz?"

"There's always places needing cooks," answered Karl, soothingly, while Mike gave him a look of disgust for encouraging the woman to stay off the subject of the murder.

"Who wants an old woman. No, Mrs. Plotz needs to be looking out for herself. No one else is going to do it for her. So, go away and let Mrs. Plotz cook and let her think maybe of what she can do to keep body and soul together."

"Damn it, woman, sit down and-we will be asking the questions," shouted Mike.

She was so startled, she did sit down and Mike commenced his interrogation.

"No, no," she said in answer to his queries, "Mrs. Plotz heard nothing the night Mr. Boylan was murdered. She was in bed sound asleep. She saw nothing and heard nothing. When a body works hard, they sleep hard." Her expression implied the police fell into a different category altogether. "Damned police, going around being hard on old widows," she mumbled.

"Your bedroom is right off the stairs leading to Boylan's second floor apartment," Weber pointed out. "How could you not have heard gunshots, or an argument, or a late arrival?"

"Hah, maybe the fella snuck in quietly. If Mrs. Plotz was plannin' to murder somebody, she wouldn't be stompin' in so everybody could hear her. And Mrs. Plotz didn't hear no gunshot neither. It's her own business she minds." The stub nose abruptly took on a life of its own and violently sniffed the air. "The beans is burnin'. See what you fellas did." She rushed to remove the pot from the stove, heaved it onto the table, and began stirring furiously to see how much was stuck to the bottom.

"Mrs. Plotz, who used the stairway besides Alderman Boylan?" demanded Mike.

"Who? Mrs. Plotz of course, the barkeeps, Duffy 'n Fitzpatrick and lots of others. Lots of folks knew he had an office up there and stayed over when it was late which was most of the time. Staying here probably gave him some peace from that 'saintly' wife of his and all her church-lovin' relatives like that brother of hers what's

runnin' the saloon into the ground. Mrs. Plotz
had to help out in her kitchen when the lady-wife
gave parties for all the priests and do-gooders in
the ward. It was always, 'Dearie me, that isn't
quite right, Mrs. Plotz.' Or 'Oh my, I wouldn't
season the stew that way, Mrs. Plotz.' She never
took a spoon to things in her kitchen that I could
see, but she sure knew how to fuss."

"How about women? Did he entertain
women upstairs?" asked Weber.

"Never," she said in a shocked voice.
"Never, that I knew, and I probably would have
had to feed them if they'd been there."

She looked fully prepared to declaim on
further grievances, but Mike had had enough and
used his thumb to motion the two of them out of
the kitchen.

In the hallway, he grumbled to Karl, "Jaysus,
that one would just repeat her ignorance of
anything but her own complaints, no matter who
was doin' the askin'. But I ain't so sure she's as
ignorant as she makes out. She's got a sly look to
her." He sighed. "Still, there's nothing to be got
from her now."

"Just show me the crime scene," said Mike,
wearily. Karl led the way upstairs. Thuds were
coming from the office, so the two men opened
the door cautiously, on guard against an intruder.

"Hi, fellas."

"What the hell are you doing here, Willie?"
asked Karl.

"Tappin' the walls for a secret panel." The
young policeman looked down. "The floors too.

The lieutenant thinks there might be a hidin'
place here somewhere."

"Found anything yet?"

"Nah." Willie grinned in his usual easygoing
way and noisily continued with his chore.

"We're here to view the scene of the crime,"
said Weber.

"Figured you was." Willie straightened up.
"I don't think there's a secret panel here
anyhow."

"You've plenty of other rooms to probe and
poke," said Mike, pointing to the door. Willie
shrugged and left. "Shite, lookin' for hidey
holes," mumbled Mike.

"The books could be important."

"They could also have been taken by the
murderer, they could be reposin' in some bank
vault, they could be at the house with Mrs.
Boylan. Damned waste of time havin' Willie
pokin' about lookin' for them." He rubbed his
face. "At least it'll keep Willie out of our hair."
He looked at Karl. "Show me the set up." This
Karl proceeded to do. Mike frowned intently at
the blood stains that had soaked into both an
expensive Persian rug and onto the wooden floor.

"We haven't let anyone in to clean the room
or change anything in it. The police have the only
keys or, at any rate, the ones that have been given
to us. We found Boylan's set in his desk but
haven't located all the locks that go with all those
keys. No one else admits to having a key to this
office."

Mike looked around the room. It was
furnished quite comfortably. Boylan didn't sleep

on a cot when staying over; he had a fully
furnished bed to one side of the room, heaped
with pillows and quilts. The covers were turned
down as if someone was going to use it any
minute, and it made Mike infinitely sad to view
it. He looked at the desk, an ornate one, carved
with all sorts of fantastic beasts and flowers.
There were even oils on the wall. Of buxom
nudes, Mike noted. One had to be Cleopatra
because she was clasping a mean-looking snake
to her bosom. Well, he thought, it's a man's
private room. And he realized, furnished to one
man's personal taste. He began surveying the
room more intently. What did it say about
Boylan?

As if he knew what Mike was thinking, Karl
pointed to the formidable lock on the door.

"Boylan opened that for his late night
visitors. He wasn't afraid that night. It couldn't
have been an obvious enemy or rival or he
wouldn't have opened the door. Or if he'd
suspected something his gun would have been
out and not stuck in the desk drawer."

"But who?"

"Maybe a woman regardless of what Mrs.
Plotz said." Karl gestured at the paintings. "The
fellow obviously liked the ladies. You heard that
from your own aunt. Moreover, he seems to have
avoided his own home. If he ran his own houses,
he could have had his pick." Seeing Mike's
frown, he added, "I said 'if.' That has yet to be
found out. Duffy and Fitzpatrick will know. They
would have guarded him there as well."

"The murderer could have been some disgruntled employee."

"Then Sloan should have known about it. He worked with Boylan long enough."

"Maybe, maybe not. But it does look like Duffy and Fitzpatrick are next on our list." He paused. "Is that a closet?"

Weber walked over to a door and pulled it open.

"We looked it over thoroughly. Check it out yourself. Boylan had good clothes. Expensive. Tasteful."

"Comin' from a snappy dresser such as yourself, that's a compliment."

"Bathhouse John should have taken lessons from him."

"Coughlan is hopeless in that department. Even his wife can't do anything about it," said Mike, as he fingered the fabrics of the numerous suits. He bent down to view the collection of boots and shoes. "He always did look good. Jaysus, what a wardrobe. I wonder if he kept as much at home."

"We didn't find any ladies' garments here. No perfume. No scents that could have indicated a female, at least not by the time we were called into the case. The locals from the precinct didn't say anything about scents either. Of course, they probably stood around puffing away on their cigars and that would have masked any perfume."

"They probably didn't notice any scents because there weren't any to notice."

"Let's go, Mike, nothing here is telling us anything. Let's interview McCarthy."

"You go sound him out. I'll join you in a few minutes. Right now I want to look the place over some more. I want to get a handle on Boylan, the private man." After Karl headed downstairs, Mike settled into Boylan's big easy chair and tried to picture the man in the selfsame spot on the fatal evening. A glass rested on the end table next to the chair, a residue of brandy still in it. There was, in fact, quite a bar on a larger table next to the wall.

Boylan must'a been sittin' here, drinkin' and smokin', mused Mike, picking up a cigar stub in a dish next to the drink. He must'a been relaxin' when a knock at the door makes him get up and let the murderer into the room. Or. . .maybe he was sittin' at the desk workin' on papers. He began looking through the letters and folders on the desk and was disappointed to find they were just ordinary contracts with various breweries and liquor interests. One folder had Fitzpatrick's name penciled in on it but that too proved innocuous. Only a reminder to have the man do a particular task.

If the Lieutenant or Karl haven't asked him what the job was, I'll do it. Might be useful. He rather doubted it though and began poking through the desk drawers. He only found stationary and envelopes. The gun was in the center drawer where it would be handy. *He couldn't have been near enough to it or he would have used it at the first hint of a threat.* Nothing in the drawer proved Boylan was an astute politician, businessman and a power to be reckoned with in the First Ward and in particular in the Levee. I wonder if the desk was cleaned out before the cops were ever called.

He turned his attention to a narrow chest of drawers. The top held toiletries, the drawers had shirts, underwear, and hose. All as neat as a pin. He'd have to talk to the Plotz woman again. Somehow she didn't look like the type to be doing valet service. A satchel under the bed showed how Boylan might have transported clean linens from home to office. *Looks like he spent more time here then at home. But damn it, the place doesn't tell me much. What did he spend his time doin' up here?* He was disappointed in Boylan somehow, the Fancy Dan clothes, the paintings, no books, just racing journals and the Police Gazette. What did I expect, he chided himself, some damned saint livin' like a monk in private? I never minded his clothes before. I liked the way he looked. As for the gamblin' and the skimmin', I knew about that and, shite it didn't bother me. So why am I havin' doubts now?

Mike locked the door with the key Willie had passed to him and headed downstairs. He decided that before joining his partner, he'd sound out Mrs. Plotz again. Grunts and exclamations from the kitchen indicated she was still on the job. He paused outside to listen. "What's Mrs. Plotz going to do?" A surprising chuckle followed her question. "Yes, she knows what to do. At least, it will be a little insurance for Mrs. Plotz."

Hearing nothing further, Mike stepped forward.

"What kind of insurance?" he asked. Startled, she shook her head and not another word could he get out of her. Shite, he said to himself, took the wrong approach and muffed it.

While Mike was musing upstairs, Karl hunted down Sloan. Before he could say anything, Sloan declared, "Mr. James J. McCarthy wants to speak to you."

"I'd like to ask him a few questions myself," said Karl. "Questioning is thirsty work, so you can bring me a beer."

Sloan nodded, and as he marched back into the main room of the saloon, he headed right for the bar to get the order. On the way, he called out, "Here's one of the cops, Mister McCarthy."

A big, beefy man with a short neck and a fat face, one of the two men who had shushed their father at the wake, turned from where he was surveying the room. His expression was sour and pinched.

That fella looks like he needs some Veronica water, mused Karl, thinking of a popular laxative sold in most saloons. One thing though, the man was well-dressed. He was wearing a blue serge suit with a faint pinstripe, a natty brocade vest and sporting an expensive gold watch and chain. A high tight celluloid collar completed his ensemble, and Karl wondered if the collar was responsible for the man's florid complexion. McCarthy 's appearance was suave enough, but he didn't look very comfortable.

Weber headed for the same corner table he and Mike had used previously. It was occupied by someone else, but the man using it left abruptly when he saw the detective advancing purposefully toward him. *Do I know him?* Karl asked himself, puzzled by the man's hasty retreat. Then he shrugged and sat down, motioning McCarthy to join him. He sat down just as Sloan approached with the beer.

Sloan was about to leave when McCarthy asked, "Has this man paid?"

"Don't be worrying, Mr. McCarthy, you aren't losing anything. I'm paying," and reaching into his pocket, Weber pulled out a nickel, holding it up so the man couldn't miss it.

"You understand," said McCarthy, "we can't be giving away the beer or how would we ever make a profit. As my da always says, 'Folks has to pay their way.' No handouts, that's our philosophy. Excuse me a minute," and the man abruptly rose and hurried over to the free lunch area of the bar.

If he can't even spring for a nickel beer, he isn't goin' to go down well at the local precinct, thought Karl. And if he doesn't know the facts of life around here, Sloan's right, he's not going to last long.

The big man returned, sat down, and explained his abrupt departure.

"Those men have got to learn that a free lunch only goes so far. That man I pulled aside had one beer and was trying to go back for free lunch a third time. We can't have that going on, the bartenders have to keep a better eye on them."

"Most saloon owners aren't that strict They know a man is sometimes down on his luck and the free lunches are all that keep him going," suggested Karl.

McCarthy ignored the advice.

"I expect it's Boylan you've come to discuss?" Karl nodded. "Good, because I'm the man to be asking. The family doesn't want you fellows bothering my sister. She's in mourning and more questions would just upset her further. She doesn't know anything about Boylan's shady dealings and doesn't need to know neither."

"And you do?"

"I know more than she does, at any rate. We, the family that is, were not happy with Patrick Boylan. My father rued the day he give her to the man. And her dowry too. Her money give him his start in this business, you know."

"Surely he's done well with it," said Karl, as he took in the spacious room. "He was an important figure on the City Council as well."

"Oh, there's no doubt he made plenty of money. . . but it's dirty money. As for holding public office, why every time we read the newspapers, he was being mentioned in some derogatory way. He gave a bad name to good Irish folks that are trying to rise from their poor beginnings. As you've undoubtedly determined by this time, he was a sinful man. Look at his friends, barflies and hustlers, gamblers and whores."

"We saw lots of important men at the wake yesterday," Karl interrupted. "Alderman Powell, Mr. Yerkes, the new Traction King, even a priest or two. Carter Harrison also came." McCarthy gave a derisive snort. Harrison was too friendly with the saloon interests for the likes of him.

"The clergy came out of deference to the widow. Boylan only contributed to the church at her urging. As for those other men you've mentioned, why they're as shady as my brother-in-law."

Karl laughed. "There isn't much to choose between them, is there?" he offered. McCarthy nodded and gave Karl the hint of a smile. The smile seemed to say that here was someone who sensibly agreed with him.

"That man," sneered McCarthy, "was rarely available for my poor sister from the first days of the marriage. We've kept most of the stuff about his gambling and other nefarious business from her, but she couldn't help hearing some of it and let me tell you, it near broke her heart. As for helping the church-say, are you a Catholic?" Karl nodded. "Well, as I said, helping the church has eased some of her pain, that and bringing up our niece to be a real lady. Still, my sister is loyal, you can't get her to bad mouth Boylan. That's a virtue, I suppose, even if her loyalty's misplaced. As God's my witness, many is the time I would have loved givin' Boylan a good drubbin', me and my brother, Joe, both."

Mike reached the table just in time to hear the last few sentences and standing over McCarthy delivered a diatribe of his own.

"If you disliked him so much, perhaps you and your brother preferred helpin' him out of this world yourselves. So, tell us, where were you two the evening Boylan was murdered?" he growled.

McCarthy turned beet red. "How dare you. We're not lawbreakers like others I could name." To emphasize his point he pounded on the table with his ham-sized fist. The resulting vibrations caused Karl's beer to slop over, and he quickly moved his chair backwards to avoid further damage to his coat. "We disapproved of Boylan, but that was as far as it went."

Karl saw Sloan staring over at them. In fact, all but the most inebriated customers were watching the show in the corner with considerable interest. McCarthy hadn't been keeping his voice down, especially not in the last exchange. He stared at Karl, saw him looking around the room, turned, and noted everyone's avid attention. He rose, and without another word, left for the rooms in the back. Slowly the atmosphere returned to normal but the obvious topic of conversation was what the two coppers had been asking that McCarthy fella because every now and then a finger was first jabbed in their direction and then in the direction of the back rooms.

"I'll bet McCarthy carried on like one of those social reformers while you two were talkin', didn't he? You can't operate a saloon with an attitude like that," complained Mike. "The damn fool, you'd think this was one of them fancy concert saloons with an orchestra and a floor show instead of a good honest place to drink a few, get a bit of sportin' news, and socialize with your fellow man. Look around you at the massage parlors, the opium dens, and the porn book stores down the street. Boylan was a saint compared to the men that run those places. And the only female on the premises is Plotz. . . and she ain't solicitin'."

Karl sat back and looked at his partner in a disgruntled way.

"Do you realize that McCarthy now knows you're prejudiced in Boylan's favor. He's not going to give you another bit of information. He's going to be hostile. We could have gotten lots more from him. In fact, I was ready to get more from him. He knew I wasn't hostile."

"Dirt was all you'd get."

"Not necessarily. Now he and his father are going to make access to the widow as difficult as possible for you." He sipped at his beer and waited for Rafferty to say something.

"She knows me; she'll talk to me." Mike didn't sound so sure though. "I'll get my aunt to help."

"It's not interrogating witnesses when you jump on everyone in defense of Boylan every time someone says something you don't like. You did it with McCarthy and with Ryan and Maxwell last night. At this rate, the only one you could interview would be his mother, that's assuming she'd have only good things to say, and if she were alive, which I know she's not." He shook his head at his partner. "Maybe you'd just better shut up and let me do the talking.

Mike sat back. He had a disgusted expression on his face, but whether at himself or at McCarthy, Karl couldn't say.

CHAPTER FIVE

"Duffy and Fitzpatrick."

Weber who was showing signs of leaving, having risen from his chair, now turned back in Rafferty's direction.

"Sit down, I'm thinking it's Duffy and Fitzpatrick we should be interviewing next. Then we can take on the gambling room employees."

"And are you going to jump on them as well for not saving Boylan? A good way to get them into an uncooperative mood and make the interview useless."

Rafferty grunted but promised not to lay into Boylan's chief errand boys and erstwhile bodyguards. He motioned over Sloan. The bartender audibly grunted, but finally, wiping his hands on his apron, approached. "Where can we find Duffy and Fitzpatrick? We need to talk to them again. We didn't get a chance at the wake, and they weren't at the funeral which was strange now that I think of it. It was kind of peculiar their missing the big send-off. "

"Dem two, they're at loose ends now." Sloan shrugged. "At a guess, they're probably holed up at their rooming house down the street, ruminating on who might need their services next. Anyway, the place is on the corner of Twenty-First and State." Satisfied he was finished with the police, he turned back to the bar.

"I'm game," said Weber. "At the first interview, they weren't very forthcoming. Maybe we asked the wrong questions."

"Well, we can ask the right ones now," declared Rafferty, pointing to the door.

The two men exited the saloon into a still less than cheery day. The weak sun had done nothing much to melt the snow which lay in soot-covered splendor all along the street, the sidewalk and next to the buildings which also exuded unpleasant vapory odors.

"When the snow first settles, it covers the debris and all of what makes this part of Chicago less than visually pleasant," mused Weber out loud. "Unfortunately, if no more falls, then there's days and days of scenes like this." Weber gestured toward the unsightly surroundings.

"It makes a fella want the cold weather gone." Rafferty looked down at his slush covered shoes. "And it's only a few days into December." He glanced over at Weber's feet sensibly clad in rubbers. "Now why didn't you remind me to wear me rubbers?"

"I thought you didn't want anyone playing

nursemaid."

Rafferty ignored the remark. "This neighborhood---no trees and bushes in their last gasp, even during the rest of the year. And look at that gloomy cigar store Indian, he feels the same way I do about the weather. The car barns over there ain't no advert either for that Chicago architecture you keep raving about. Only the bordellos on Dearborn try for a bit more style."

"Especially the Everleigh Club."

Mike stopped, "Here's the rooming house. Which don't look too bad," he said, pointing to a red-brick building of three stories with an entrance up a short flight of stairs. Confronted by a front door unfortunately painted in a garish green color, he added, "Put a red bow on that and the place will do nicely for Christmas." He led the way inside, and unlike the usual rooming house, this one had a front desk complete with a squirt of a clerk. "Looks more like a hotel than a rooming house."

They both looked around in surprise. Whoever had done the door, had done the lobby as well. The front desk was as garishly green as the front door and the rest of the room was done in red floral for the sofas, gold floral for the chair upholstery, and scattered here and there were rugs with lively paisley designs.

"Well, if the neighborhood was drab, this place is tryin' its best to make up for it. It isn't the Palmer House, but it's kind of welcoming." Both men grinned at the display. In addition, there were the usual potted plants, remarkably healthy specimens, as well as tables with newspapers and magazines. Except for the squirt, this lively little universe was otherwise empty of life.

"What can I do for you gentlemen?"

"You can tell us whether Brian Duffy and Kevin Fitzpatrick are here and if they are, tell us where they are." Weber and Rafferty both held up their badges.

"I bet I know what that's about. You're in luck. They've nuthin' better to do than hang around here." And the squirt pointed in the direction of another room off the front foyer.

Rafferty and Weber entered a sort of parlor with tables, more sofas and chairs, and a color scheme involving yellow and orange this time. They saw Duffy and Fitzpatrick playing cards, but in an obviously disinterested and aimless way. Still looking around, Rafferty commented, "This is quite the place you've been livin' in. Pretty lively decor."

"And guess whose it is," chuckled Duffy.

"Not Boylan's?"

The men nodded.

"At least the McCarthys won't be tossin us' out of here anytime soon, the fookers." Duffy paused. "Ah, but youse fellas are just here needin' more information." Duffy it seemed was to be the spokesman for the two of them, Fitzpatrick remaining mute.

For a few moments, they all stared at one another. Rafferty was surprised at their appearance. Whenever he'd seen them before, they'd looked well turned out even at the wake-though somewhat garishly in Duffy's case, but not now. They'd quickly acquired a seedy look.

"We missed you at the funeral. I would have thought you two would want to pay your last respects."

"We was warned off in mighty strong language by the Brothers McCarthy," Duffy replied, and Fitzpatrick nodded in agreement.

"You were at the wake," pointed out Weber.

"We was nearly thrown out, but we stood our ground. I guess the McCarthys didn't want to make a fuss in front of all those respectable mourners. But afterwards, they gave us our marchin' orders. We weren't to show our faces at the church or at the cemetery. "Yeah," he added, "we aren't even welcome in the saloon. If we show up, we'll be tossed out."

Mike having taken a dislike to the McCarthys, found himself in sympathy with the two men. "And why do they have this beef with you?"

Fitzpatrick answered, "They disliked Boylan, and we were his men. So. . .they don't want to see the likes of us. What's that fancy term? Yeah, we're persona non grata." Then he smiled, "Still, our connection to Boylan may be openin' some doors."

"But not soon enough," groused Duffy. "Leastwise, we can stay here for the time being, this being Boylan's place. and us living here rent free."

"Why are you safe from the McCarthys here?" asked Weber.

"Ah, the Alderman has. . . had, buildings all over the Levee, and the McCarthys won't be

knowing about them anytime soon. Now if
Boylan had been dying of some ailment, he
might have mentioned these other properties, you
know for his missus and Maureen, but, as things
stand, they'll have fun ferreting out everything he
owned. The McCarthys didn't like Boylan, but he
disliked them just as much."

Duffy nodded agreement at Fitzpatrick's
summary.

"In the meantime you can help us," declared
Rafferty. "We've got lots more questions.
Weber, here, tells me you fellas weren't very
forthcoming last time."

"Yeah, well we wanted to spare the widow.
We didn't know how mean that family was
gonna be. We ain't gonna spare them now. So
ask away, boys", invited Duffy.

"We want to know about all the visitors
Boylan might have had traipsing in and out of his
private quarters at the saloon. Anyone he might
have had up there that could have done him in?
Any women?"

Both men laughed. "No women, fellas."

"But to the McCarthys, Boylan was playing
around."

Fitzpatrick pointed a finger at Rafferty. "He
never had a woman up in his office." Then he
looked cockily at the two detectives. "He was a
regular at the Everleigh Club. He was one of
Minna's best-paying customers. And we got to sit
in the back with her own staff, pass the time, and
eat out-of-this-world food too. French. In fact,
the two of us are hoping to get taken on by the
Everleigh sisters."

"We hope," said Duffy but he looked doubtful. "Well, maybe you, Fitz, you got more learning. He's always reading books, he is," and looking at his partner, "and using words like that there persona non grata. Me, I ain't got that kinda class."

"The Everleighs don't need you to entertain the guests," retorted Fitzpatrick. "Just to bounce, discreetly of course, anyone getting rowdy. And you can sure do that." He gestured to Duffy's tough frame for the benefit of the detectives.

"So the Everleigh Club is another place we need to go and interview folks. That could be interesting. I'm looking forward to it," Weber declared. "It's famous or infamous. Either way, it'll be a new experience for the two of us. But they're fairly new. What about back some time?"

After looking at Fitzpatrick and getting a nod, Duffy admitted, "He set up a lady in her own place before the Everleighs come to town. But we don't know anythin' about that. We didn't do no guardin' for those visits. Don't even know the location."

Weber and Rafferty exchanged looks. Here was something else that they had to look into, but how to get the information might be a problem. They'd figure that out later. Meanwhile Boylan must have had other enemies. Disgruntled constituents for example. "What about enemies right here in the ward? Angry constituents," suggested Weber.

"Yeah, the day I got sick, there was that Knobby. He threatened Boylan. I saw you two go all tense."

"That was an automatic reaction. You saw how easily Knobby backed down. No, his sort don't go killin' the goose that laid the golden egg."

Rafferty jabbed a finger at Fitzpatrick. "Then why did he keep a gun handy?"

"Come on, you two. This is the Levee. You know that some fellas can get into it right in the street. So a gun is extra insurance. And the muggers. Don't tell me you don't know about our muggers. So, yeah, Boylan had a gun on the premises. Bathhouse John and Hinky Dink Kenna probably do too. But you won't see them tremblin' in their shoes or hidin' out at home. Neither did Boylan. And no we haven't heard of anyone with a personal beef against him, except for the McCarthys."

Rafferty shrugged. "You two are founts of information but maybe the Everleigh sisters will be more help, so why don't the two of you get your act together and escort us down there. You can introduce us."

Fitzpatrick and Duffy looked doubtful. "It's not as if we ever had any dealings with the Everleighs. We were just there with Boylan. We left him at the front door and went around to the back ourselves. Heck, we don't even know what the front lobby looks like. Boylan did give us a description of the splendors on view for paying guests, and believe me, those folks, they're paying through the nose. That place ain't cheap. Yeah, Boylan told us lots. He was impressed himself with the way those two run the club. . . and he'd seen a lot. Well, he told us. He could unload on us. He sure couldn't with his in-laws. And Hinky Dink Kenna and Bathhouse John know all about the Club. Heck, dem two sisters help support the police department and are in cahoots with as many politicos as have influence for sale. And don't think Boylan didn't do what he could to protect them."

Duffy's long comment left Rafferty even more disillusioned with Boylan, But what did I expect, he mused. "He had gambling on his premises. I suspected he bought votes. I knew that, so why wouldn't he be protecting bordellos in his ward and expecting a payback? Aloud he asked, "Did he keep bordellos himself."

"Nah, he did not," said Fitzpatrick with considerable vehemence in his voice.

After casting a triumphant smile at Weber, Rafferty made a shooing motion with his hands in the direction of Duffy and Fitzpatrick, "Get yourselves shaved, put on something that doesn't look like you've slept in it, and then get yourselves back here. The four of us are going to the Everleigh Club and to the back door, if necessary, to inquire if the sisters want to help us solve Boylan's murder. I expect they'll be only too happy to assist." Mike turned to his partner, "We can do the last employees after the Everleighs. They sound more promising anyway."

The two unemployed men acknowledged that showing up at the Club and looking like they were still loyal to their old boss wasn't a bad idea and headed upstairs. The two detectives leaned back in order to be reasonably comfortable while they waited, Weber cocking his head and examining his partner. Becoming aware of his partner's scrutiny, Rafferty demanded, "Why're you staring at me? Have I suddenly developed spots or what?"

"No, no, but I've something to ask. My family would like to meet you; so I'm inviting you to a holiday dinner. Maybe the Sunday before Christmas. I'll borrow my brother's rig and pick you up. No sense in exposing you to the elements when you were so recently laid low."

"Let me get this straight, your family wants to meet me?"

"Well, I've mentioned you often enough. Besides, we've things in common. We went to the same prep school, though you were ahead of me by a couple of years. I assure you they'll greet you as my friend." Karl was secretly crossing his fingers as he hadn't as yet consulted the family. But he knew that they didn't have any animosity toward the Irish, in general, though they were not admirers of men like Powell or Coughlin. Or Boylan for that matter. After all, both the Irish *and* the Germans were fairly recent immigrants and had had to struggle to move upward socially. And Karl did mention his partner often and in a favorable light.

"This is certainly a surprise," answered Mike and after considering the matter for a few moments, "I guess I accept. I've heard enough about your family to be curious myself. Heck, this Christmas, Aunt Maggie and I were even planning on putting up a Christmas tree and for that custom I guess we have to thank you fellas.

Don't know though if I like the idea of lighting candles all over it. Seems a bit risky."

The Christmas invitation and its friendly reception put both men into good spirits and improved their view of Duffy and Fitzpatrick when the two came back into the room. "There, you fellas look much better now," said Rafferty, scrutinizing them closely. "You don't seem to be packin."

"Nah, Fitz here tossed his gun when he heard." This remark by Duffy earned him a glare which was ignored. "Said he was goin' to throw it in the Sanitary Channel or Bubbly Creek. Hell, I followed along, I was that afraid he'd jump in after the gun, seein' what a shock he'd had. Sloan hisself came to tell us the news and one of the first things Fitz did was throw his gun against the wall and curse on how useless he and his weapon were. Though we weren't there, so it wasn't on us. Right?"

"If you'd been dismissed by Boylan for the night, of course not," agreed Weber.

"What kind of gun was it?" asked Rafferty.

"A Colt 45. We both packed 45s. Boylan got 'em for us." Rafferty exchanged glances with Weber. They'd been fairly sure from Boylan's wound that it was a Colt 45 bullet that did it for him. Yet how could Fitzpatrick who obviously idolized Boylan have had anything to do with his death?

"Anyways, if he was gonna throw himself after the gun, I was there to stop it. But he didn't." Fitzpatrick still looked put out. "But the gun's gone. And considerin' what's in those waters, it's probably mush by now." Bubbly Creek as everyone knew was an especially lethal body of water, if it could even be called water what with its sinister toxic burps a constant. And the Canal wasn't much better.

"Where's your Colt, Duffy?" asked Weber.

"Upstairs. We sure won't need it at the Everleigh Club."

The detectives rose and indicated that Duffy and Fitzpatrick should lead the way for the short distance to the Club.

CHAPTER SIX

Outside the snow had begun to fall, but gently. As it drifted silently into each nook and cranny, it softened the hard and ugly lines, and threw a mantle over soot and stain. The Levee looked pure and white.

As the men stood in front of the two Everleigh buildings on south Dearborn, Weber said, "It's ironic, Mike, but at Purcell's mansion, we marched in the front door, yet at a bordello, we're only welcome at the back. Good enough for the one, but not quite the thing for the other. You two show us the way, introduce us, and we'll see to it we meet the sisters." He paused to examine the front facade: three stories, a double entrance, and plenty of windows. Then, abruptly, he started for the stairs.

"We're going in the front. The hell with timidly creeping around to the rear entrance. The sisters should be glad to see us. If they really liked Boylan, they'll be eager to help. They'll want to be seen as helping our investigation."

Before Weber had a chance to ring the bell more than once, the door opened. Confronted by what looked like a rather posh butler, Weber stated their business and both detectives displayed their badges.

"Gentlemen you are welcome. Believe me, the Misses Everleigh are eager to be of assistance." He saw Rafferty glance to the bottom of the stairs, saw Duffy and Fitzpatrick and with a simple gesture of his thumb motioned the two of them around to the back. "Boylan's men can wait for you where they've always waited for the Alderman, 'round back. Please gentlemen." And he indicated they should enter what proved to be a spacious hallway. "Wait here, and I will inform the Misses Everleigh of your presence." At the same time, he pointed to well-cushioned sofas and chairs of which they had their choice. "It may take a bit of time. Divest yourselves of those heavy coats and mufflers. We enjoy a comfortable temperature in here that does not go with heavy outdoor clothing."

Rafferty and Weber did just that, piling their coats on a chair and seating themselves side by side on one of the sofas. From their vantage point they silently admired the room: grand staircases and plenty of thriving greenery with statues of classical beauties peeping through, the kind of classical beauties that prep school boys hunted down in books on Greek history and art. Persian rugs and a parquet floor. Everything that was both gracious and grand seemed to be on display.

"That fella was right. It's downright tropical in here. And for the two of us, it was sure a nice

reception. No bum's rush here." Rafferty sniffed.
"I'm smelling flowers. Even all the bouquets at
the wake didn't come across like this." In silence,
they could see mahogany staircases winding their
way elegantly upstairs to who knows what added
delights.

They sat until the rustle of petticoat and skirt
indicated the presence of one of the sisters. As
the men rose, she introduced herself as Minna
Everleigh. "And you are?"

"Detectives Karl Weber and Michael
Rafferty of the City Hall Detective Squad
commanded by Lieutenant Steele. The case has
been taken out of the hands of the local police as
it is definitely a high priority. There is a lot of
pressure for a solution to the crime. And we only
learned today, through Duffy and Fitzpatrick, that
Alderman Boylan frequented your club."

"Yes, he was a regular, a welcome regular."
Turning to her butler, if that is what he was, she
asked him to see to coffee for the detectives and
some cakes and savory sandwiches as well. Both
men had risen on her entrance, but she then
motioned them to be seated. "This may take a bit
of time, Officers."

Weber sat but began describing what they
needed. "This is a bit awkward, Miss Everleigh,"
he said. "We hope to know anything Alderman
Boylan might have let drop here to you or your
staff or the other guests that may show us a way
to move forward at finding if he had any
enemies. . . persons seriously meaning him harm.
In fact we need to know more about the man. The

more we know, the sooner we'll have a solution."

"I will certainly and personally interview my staff, and if I find something promising, you will be allowed a face-to-face interrogation yourselves. We can't of course allow you to be here when guests are present. It would be very disruptive and what we provide is the opposite-a pleasant evening visiting our ladies, or dining with friends. You know it isn't only the young ladies that draw our guests but in equal amounts, I believe, it is for gentlemen to talk over an exquisitely prepared dinner, with drinks, and cigars and, in general, to enjoy good camaraderie. Deals, too, I believe have been made, of a business or political nature, over a pleasant evening here at the Club. Alderman Boylan enjoyed both sorts of evenings here. He was, as Fitzpatrick and Duffy must have told you, a regular. We saw him perhaps once a week. The rest of the time I assume was taken up with affairs at city hall and in his own ward. He also supported us when we needed advice. Mr. John Coughlin, Alderman Powell and Mr. McKenna and others did the same."

"So there'll be no interviews for us today?"

"Not until I have my own first. We are discreet you understand." This Weber did not precisely understand because the Sisters Everleigh were known to toot their own horn rather often and loudly. As if reading his mind, she added, "Discreet as far as our guests and their activities, of course."

"Ah, here's the coffee and a bit of food as well. We are very well known for our cuisine.

Some men, indeed, come for the dining experience. I do believe I shall leave you to it. Simpson can, after you have refreshed yourselves, give you a tour of some of our lovely rooms if you so wish." She left in a further swish of skirts.

"Gentlemen, may I pour you our coffee? We serve an excellent imported brew here at the Everleigh Club."

"Thank you, yes," replied Weber.

"I won't hover. Enjoy your repast, and I'll return and hopefully conduct you on that tour Miss Minna promised." He strode silently away.

"I'm gob-smacked, Karl. Could the Queen of England be dealt with more graciously? The only thing missin' was a curtsey."

It was a considerable time later that the two men left the Everleigh Club. Once the door was shut behind them, Rafferty staggered to one side and groped at the entrance wall. "Give me a hand, Karl. I'm stunned into paralysis-Gold room, Egyptian room, Chinese, Silver, Copper, Red, Rose, Green, and Blue. Pennants, gold spittoons, blue leather pillows with Gibson girls all over 'em, fountains. I'll never recover." He paused. "Though they slipped up a bit in the taste department on that one statue. I don't think a Greek goddess normally has a clock in her stomach." They both laughed. Then Mike sniffed his coat sleeve. "And Jaysus, I smell like a gardenia. What are you waitin' for, Karl? Help me down the stairs. Me feet won't support me."

"I never suspected you had a flair for the dramatic, Mike."

"I'm pulverized and do I get any help from you? No not a bit." Both men burst into laughter.

"It was rather too much," admitted Weber. "But it seems customers are lining up eager to toss fifty bills a night at the Misses Everleigh, so they're doing something right. You know for fifty dollars you can go to Europe first class. And it's probably true that they're getting a national reputation and receiving wealthy foreigners as well, or our tour guide wouldn't have dropped all those names. After all, detectives with our skills could easily find out if all that was really true."

"Well, maybe that showboater Gentleman Jim Corbett was a visitor, but John L. Sullivan, him I can't picture on those premises. Ah, Karl, it's too cold out here to be conversin'. Let's see to Duffy and Fitzpatrick and then go report this new development to Steele."

"Yeah", Weber winked, "he might want to investigate this new opening into Boylan's murder himself." They did see the bodyguards as well, but merely to dismiss them. "We still got the gambling side of the saloon to interview but that can wait. Steele will want an update." So the two got themselves to police headquarters. Lieutenant Steele gave a small smile at the news, but didn't seem as enthusiastic to introduce himself into that part of the investigation as Weber and Rafferty had assumed. "I'd rather leave the interviews at the Everleigh Club to you fellows." He sighed. "Ah, boys, the Columbian Exposition is getting close. We're already under strong pressure to clean up the city. 'Shut down all the blind pigs. Winkle out all the panel houses and close them down. Close the bordellos and gambling dens,' say the powers that be. Though how can we do that when some of our most prominent politicians run the gambling dens out of their saloons and protect the bordellos?

" 'Clean up the city,' say the Palmers and the Fields. No, I've got enough on my plate as it is. This has been a year! And as if we don't have enough law-breakers of our own, anyone with train fare arrived here from the rest of the country to clean up at the Democratic Convention last summer. And they're staying over for the Fair."

"I thought that Detective Wooldridge out of the Harrison Street Station was doing wonders."

"He is, he is, but we need a troop of Wooldridges and not all of us have his flair for disguises. The fellow can be a rancher from the West come to see the big city or a naive mid-Western farmer ready to be fleeced. God, I wish we had more like him. You two know the pressure I'm getting from City Hall.

"Boylan, as important as he was, is no longer my top priority. But he is still yours. As for you, Mike," Steele pointed a finger in Rafferty's direction, "it seems Boylan's lawyer wants to see you at the earliest opportunity. Here's the address, the name, business hours, etc. So get yourself down there."

"What does his lawyer want to see me for?" squawked Rafferty, who'd drunk in wariness of the legal profession along with his mother's milk.

"You'll just have to go and see," said Steele dismissively and nodded toward the door.

Outside, Rafferty continued to fume and fuss

finally declaring, "Karl, come with me. The man's firm is in the Rookery. You can offer support."

"Why would you need support? Is anyone suing you?"

"Of course not-I think. Anyway, be a pal and come along. An early supper's on me."

Weber shrugged, but in the end, acquiesced. Once inside the building, it was discovered that the lawyer in question was on an upper floor and the two men had to take an elevator. Rafferty grunted.

"You've got to get over your timidity about heights and elevators."

"Easy for you to say. Oh, hell, let's get it over with before I turn tail."

The lawyer's firm, with an impressive string of names on the office door, was finally reached. Upon entering what was a rather affluent establishment, they were instantly and courteously greeted by a clerk.

"Detective Sergeant Rafferty to see Lawyer Beagle. I apologize for not callin' ahead but I just got the news and happened to be in the vicinity."

"Ahem, yes, lawyer Baggle. Of course, I'll see if he's available." And the clerk selecting one of several impressive doors, entered, and after a pause reappeared and motioned both men into an office lined with a reassuring array of what were presumably legal tomes. The furniture-massive desk and comfortable chairs-also spoke of someone who knew his business or at least profited from it.

Lawyer Baggle addressed Rafferty. "Ah, yes,

Sergeant, please, you and your associate be
seated." He buzzed the outer office and the clerk
reappeared. "Get the Boylan file. This will only
take a moment. Alderman Boylan's file is one of
our top priorities right now. Ah, here's the file."
Baggle paged through the papers, finally
announcing, "Here we are. Sergeant Rafferty you
are the recipient of a legacy from Alderman
Boylan." He smiled. "I see this comes as a
surprise." Rafferty looked stunned, unable to do
anything after his initial gasp expect to stare.

Baggle once again buzzed the outer office
and upon the return of the clerk asked for a glass
of water for the Sergeant.

"You obviously had no idea about this
bequest." He handed over an envelope. "The
amount is in here, and so you can collect,
instructions are given."

All Rafferty could do while gulping down
the water was shake his head.

"He also left a letter for you." Baggle handed
it over. "The Alderman was most generous. He
could afford to be. Why, what he's left to his
widow and to his daughter will keep them in
comfort forever especially if she takes our advice
and sells at least some of her properties. Because
of the Fair, properties in the right places are
fetching a high price. Moreover Alderman
Boylan held properties all over the Levee."

"Yes, we saw some of them including an
attractive hotel on Twenty-First and State,"
contributed Weber.

"A hotel on Twenty-First and State?"

Weber backtracked, "More like a rooming

house maybe."

"This is news to me. Maybe the widow and I
do not have a full list of all the Alderman's
properties. Yes, that's possible. After all, his
death was unexpected and so his will wasn't
complete. That means further research will be
necessary on our part. Well, gentlemen, I won't
detain you any further." Once again the front
office was buzzed, the clerk reappeared, and the
two detectives were courteously escorted off the
premises.

Back in the street, Rafferty turned to Weber,
"Karl, I think you let the cat out o' the bag
mentioning that hotel."

"Yeah, sorry about that."

"Still, it's got nothing to do with us. I
promised you a meal, and it seems I now may
even have the means to pay for it. And I can read
my mail while we eat."

They adjourned to a nearby German
establishment that Weber recommend. Seated,
served, and drinking their first beer, Rafferty
opened the letter from Boylan, even though he
could see Weber was more interested in learning
about the bequest.

"To my dear Michael." Rafferty quickly read
through the letter. "I'll summarize it for you,
Karl. Boylan goes on and on about what good
pals he was with both my folks and my aunt and
uncle. Aunt Maggie told you how he helped
when my uncle set himself up in the saloon
business and that that's what put them on the
road to prosperity. He also says he regrets not

helping more with me. Well, in those early days, he had more knowledge than means. And Karl, he really did help me. He's how I got on the detective squad because, by that time, he was well-to-do and influential himself. Anyway, he goes on to say he'd have liked a son like me."

Rafferty paused and sighed.

"Ah, I should have seen him more than I did." He looked down at the lengthy letter. "He goes on about my Aunt Maggie as well."

Weber nodded.

"Is that it? Then for heaven's sake get to the amount of the bequest."

This time Rafferty was only able to produce a squeak and handed Baggle's letter to Weber, who replied with a "Good grief. Sorry, grief is an inappropriate word under the circumstances. What a sum! You can go shopping today on your expectations. After all you're now one of the haves."

"Never," Rafferty snorted. "I'll never feel like a have. I've been careful all me life and that's not going to change now." He slapped the table. "Karl, we've got to find the killer and make him pay. I felt bad about Boylan's death before, and now I feel it more than ever. I owe him twice over. Let's get back to headquarters and see what other trails we can follow."

At headquarters, Steele informed them that the following day they could do the interviewing at the Everleigh Club at ten in the morning. "The sisters got back to us quickly, I must say. They're obviously eager to help. They're taking this request very seriously. For now, go home. Oh say, Rafferty, did you see the lawyer? I heard it might have been a legacy."

"I'll be able to stand Karl here a few lunches at last and maybe get myself a new hat," Rafferty answered quickly.

"Oh, well, that's good, Mike." He pointed to the door, "Go and get yourselves that meal and then go home. Tomorrow will probably be a long day for both of you."

Once outside the office, Mike told Karl that the legacy amount was just between the two of them, "I don't think Steele or anyone else around here has to know the size of the legacy. I don't want to cause any envy."

"That's only common sense. I won't mention it to anyone." They also agreed to meet at the Everleigh Club at ten on the following day.

CHAPTER SEVEN

The two detectives were once again cordially received at the Everleigh Club, but the interviews again proved only minimally useful. However, from a waiter in the elegant dining room, they did get a list of Boylan's dinner companions. But these proved to have been political allies and hardly the types that would want to see Boylan done in. Moreover, even Boylan's favorite young lady didn't have anything useful to share. She impressed both men with both her looks and demeanor. They could see why Boylan found her especially attractive. She bubbled with vitality. Laughter seemed to come easily to her. Sunny, some would have called her.

"He didn't go in for pillow talk, you know. Gossip, I mean. Oh, he'd tell some funny stories about folks in his ward. Folks he'd meet at his saloon. One was about a fella that saw giant rabbits or horses or some such when the poor soul was in his cups. And near Halloween,

Alderman Boylan gave me a bit of a fright telling
me about banshees. But he certainly didn't
discuss business, political or otherwise. In fact,"
said the young lady, who'd introduced herself as
Eva, short for Evangelina, seemed quite proud of
this. "He liked to hear about my people and
where I'd come from and that was a first, believe
me." She was clever enough to see the two
detectives were disappointed. "Sorry."

"Not your fault. No one else has much to say
either." Eva didn't seem in any hurry to get away
and began scrutinizing them more closely. She
smiled briefly, then shrugged in what appeared to
be disappointment.

We've met with her approval, thought Karl,
but alas, we're not financially up to snuff. Still,
she seemed reluctant to leave.

"Say fellas, I got a question of my own.
What's going to happen to Kevin now?"

"What? Kevin Fitzpatrick, him that was
Boylan's bodyguard?"asked Rafferty. She
nodded. "He's a grown man, he'll just get
another job."

"But he was so devoted to Alderman Boylan.
And Kevin's was such a hard luck story, and
Boylan helped him out." Both detectives were
curious now and urged her to continue.

"I'm not gossiping, you know. And well, us
girls think Kevin's a nice looking fellow and feel
sorry for him. Also this is common knowledge.
Poor Kevin, you know, was born in a whore
house and who knows who his father was. For
being so careless, his mother could have been
thrown out, but Toots Sweeney was a bit of a

softy and put her to workin' in the laundry. The baby when it showed up became a sort of pet or mascot though it was kept well away from the customers.

I wasn't here at the time, you understand. My god, that was ages ago, but I've heard that Toots did say that if anyone else got pregnant she'd be out on her ear. I guess her charity only went so far. Well, Kevin's mother was an Irish lass, sadly gone astray." This coming from Eva seemed a strange observation. She certainly didn't act as if she'd gone astray.

"Alderman Boylan came to hear of this, oh, maybe when Kevin was about seven and offered to send him to parochial school - paid for him until he was about thirteen. After that, Kevin went to work running errands for Toots and for Boylan. When he got old enough, he was taken on as a bodyguard. So you see Boylan's always been there. And now. . .?"

"Who actually knows this story? You've only heard it secondhand, right?" Weber peered at the girl.

Eva had to give that some thought. "Toots is gone now but some of her old crew still work in our kitchens and laundry. Old Daisy would be one of those. And she was there on the spot."

"Ask if we can interview her as well."

"Sure."

Daisy was available and looked happy to be away from pots and pans even if for only a short time. She confirmed everything Eva had said and added details.

"Kevin probably got the Alderman's

attention because him and his mum were Irish. Now me, I'm Scots-Irish, and I'll bet, he'd niver help the likes of me. Charity only goes so far. Anyways, the Alderman was somethin' special to Kevin." She stopped, "That's all I know." The two men thanked and dismissed her.

"No wonder Kevin took Boylan's murder so badly. Well, I hope the poor sod lands on his feet," said Karl sympathetically. Mike concurred. "We aren't really any further ahead on our investigation though. I really thought we'd do better."

"Yeah, too bad he didn't discuss something besides Pookas and banshees with Evangelina." They thanked Minna Everleigh personally but did mention their frustration, which she noted with sympathy.

"If I learn anything more at all I'll be sure and contact your Lieutenant Steele." She paused. "I'm truly sorry we weren't able to help. You know, it's close to the dinner hour. We've got a small private room for dining. Why don't I tell my chef to rustle up a meal and the wine's on me as well. Maybe that'll cheer you two up." She smiled at them. "And us business women. . . why, we do try to stay on good terms with the police. So what do you say?" Both men instantly agreed.

They were shown to the small private room, were seated, and served with wine. The dinner, when it came, was excellent.

"French," declared Karl, stabbing at a garlicky snail which Mike was regarding with some apprehension.

"What do you think of the girls at the club, Mike?"

"They're younger and nicer than I expected. I've heard plenty of so-called good women call them scarlet women, harlots, and worse. But they don't seem callous or brazen, not really. For instance, that Evangelina, she appreciated Boylan's asking about her back story, her folks and her tastes. Of course, we've known hard types who wouldn't think twice about slippin' someone knock-out drops, and then helping some male partner strip the sucker down to his unmentionables. And they aid and abet in the panel house racket. I just get a different impression of the ladies here. I guess I can call them 'ladies' though me Aunt Maggie wouldn't agree."

"Just proves you shouldn't rush to judgment."

"Still and all, I don't think I'd ever use. . . ah, the services here. You know, you're lucky, you've got a mother and two sisters. You probably know what makes a woman tick. I've never been close to any woman except Aunt Maggie, and she's usually too busy to talk, always has been. And going to prep and all-no girls. Aunt Maggie's never paraded nice Irish girls past me either. Don't know if I'd like her matchmaking anyhow. What about you? How's your love life?"

Karl said nothing.

"You're not still hanging out with that woman you met on the Purcell case? Jaysus,

Karl, she's married."

"Not for much longer. The paperwork's already been done. Mrs. Purcell has been encouraging her all this while, and soon she'll be free of that abuser. . . and her name is Caroline."

"What does your family think? I'll wager you haven't told them."

"As soon as she's divorced, there won't be any further impediment."

"That far along is it? Don't tell me you're making wedding plans."

"Listen, Mike, we're done talking on the subject, though I'll tell you that I am seeing her, though not nearly enough. I do know she can stay on with Mrs. Purcell if she wishes. She isn't going back to her family. She blames them for rushing her into the marriage with Fielding in the first place. They thought her marriage would help them socially."

"How are you going to support somebody who's used to a comfortable life at the home of a Gold Coast widow?"

"No more discussion. Let's finish up and get going."

"Suits me."

Outside Mike wondered what they should try next.

"Maybe that fellow that worked on the gambling side, what was his name? Yeah, Charlie Pike." He gave the matter a moment's more thought. "Nah, how about our favorite reporter. He'll be easier enough to find." But Maxwell had been sent out to cover a coup of

Officer Wooldridge's. That officer had managed
to get the upper hand over a gang of pickpockets
operating along Wabash avenue on the street
cars. He and his men had cornered the whole
gang, secured their lair, and learned they'd also
been working the big stores on State Street which
made the coup even more impressive.

"The gambling manager it is. What's his
location?" asked Weber.

"It's back to the Levee for Mr. Charlie Pike."
Pike's place of residence wasn't bad. Perhaps
even a bit of an improvement over the hotel
Duffy and Fitzpatrick called home. They were
lucky to find Pike was in residence. He proved to
be a short thin man who looked remarkably like a
fish. His name fit perfectly.

"We've never interviewed any of the
gamblin' house staff."

"What gamblin' staff?" demanded Pike.

"Oh, come off it. We all know that gambling
was goin' on. We're not here to arrest you, fella.
We're just investigatin' the death of Boylan and
need as much information as possible. Can you
help us? What did you see and hear on the night
in question?"

"If you know that gamblin' was going on,
you should also know we were in a separate
building. What went on in the saloon and in
Boylan's private room was none of our business.
I certainly heard nothing myself. All of us on that
side discussed the murder, but none of us saw or
heard a thing. So save yourself from interviewing
the rest of the men. You should also know we
were open late and still wheelin' and dealin'. We

were still busy. It's amazing how determined gamblers are to lose their money. I guess it's true that hope springs eternal."

"Did they know about any enemies Boylan might have had?"

Pike actually considered that for a few minutes.

"Oh, there's some that disliked him, like the McCarthys. I heard about them all right from Sloan. Some politicians maybe too. But it was only dislike not hate, not enough to murder him. You know, I'm glad I don't have to solve your mystery. I wouldn't know where to look neither. I personally liked working for Boylan. Now, we're all temporarily out of jobs though it won't be for long. We'll have to scatter, but we'll all find a place soon enough. Plenty of gamblin' still going on."

"Could anyone have gone through from the saloon side to your side that evening."

"Not that I noticed-I told you." Weber and Rafferty finally gave up.

Outside Weber said, "Another dead end."

"What next?"

"Headquarters."

By the time Rafferty and Weber got back to headquarters, they were downright depressed about their own case. "Maybe Aunt Maggie knows something more. Or we can re-interview Mrs. Plotz, I still think she knows more than she's telling." Mike paused. "It's just hard to believe Boylan was such a loner in the middle of all that camaraderie. A man's got to have someone to talk to doesn't he? He can't bottle it all up, can he?"

"I don't know. Not everyone is like Bathhouse John. I certainly don't tell my folks everything about work. In fact, I tell them very little because they're always ragging me about being in the police. Being a lawyer or a doctor, a professor of something or other, that's fine. But policing. No. Yet all these new innovations in crime detection are making policing more than a job; it can be a career, a profession. Anyway, that's what I keep telling my grandfather, brother, and father. And that's another reason for your Christmas invitation. You're going to help me make my point by being yourself." He scrutinized Rafferty. "But for the evening, at least, leave the brogue at home. Some of them, why their English isn't that good, my mother and grandfather for instance; they aren't up to understanding a dialect as well. And for the ones with good English, please don't drop all those gs."

Mike decided not to be offended because he knew he put on an Irish flavor sometimes just for the hell of it. The two men parted on good terms with plans to meet the next day at the Globe after first ascertaining if their favorite reporter, Maxwell, was finally in residence.

Maxwell was indeed at his desk. "You're here to get some help on the Boylan case, aren't you?" They nodded. "And what do I get in return?"

Weber and Rafferty had already consulted on

this and had decided that what they had could be
shared with Maxwell because it was hardly
anything to be secretive about.

"We found out he was a regular at the
Everleigh Club."

"I already knew that. Anything else?" Seeing
their disappointment, he added, "You can at least
stand me to some food. Yeah, you feed me, and
I'll feed you. And let's not eat just anywhere.
Pick a good spot." He tapped the side of his nose,
a gesture Weber recognized as belonging to
someone about to impart wisdom and which
again made him wonder what the side of one's
nose had to do with vital information.

Rafferty deferred to Weber on the subjects of
restaurants.

"Well, there's Schlogl's where you can get
baked owl." Both Rafferty and Maxwell mimed
barfing.

"Buffalo steak at Kinsley's?"

"You're getting warmer but try again"
Maxwell grinned.

"The Union Restaurant over on Randolph for
the greatest collection of cold cuts available."

"Now you're talking." Maxwell quickly
donned heavy coat, mufflers, mittens, a hat that
looked like it had denuded a bear, and rubbers.
"I'm ready. Bring on the cable car. Your treat as
well." He stabbed a finger in the air. "But never
fear, because I do have something for you fellas."

The three of them waited in the cold, too
long they all felt. They began stamping their feet
in imitation of the policeman directing traffic
who must surely have felt worse than they did

under his coal-shuttle helmet.

"Does the poor fellow at least have earmuffs?" queried Maxwell.

"He does," reassured Weber.

"And thank the Lord, here's our transportation," murmured Rafferty, pointing to the cable car with its grip man. "There's another fellow who's stuck outside in the freezing cold." The man in question was wrapped in a huge fur coat with a fur hat, ears muffed and hands protected by thick gloves with gauntlets.

Weber and Rafferty hustled Maxwell out of the frigid air and into a noxious atmosphere of bad breath, sour mud, and soiled clothing. Only a bit less than whole rows of people stood up determinedly holding on to straps as the car lurched along.

"At least we're not with the crowd rushing home."

The grip must have seized the cable because the car suddenly lunged forward. If the passengers hadn't been so firmly attached to their straps, they could have sailed up front or all the way back or directly to the floor, which was a fate from which they all prayed to be spared.

Reaching the Union Restaurant, the three men were happily transported intact to a Munich Rathskeller. They sniffed happily while divesting themselves of heavy outerwear. A waiter seated them and presented the menu. "Their Wiener Schnitzel Union is the specialty of the house, that's a veal cutlet cooked in Madeira or something. But their cold cut tray is what's really spectacular. It comes on a tray four feet long and three feet wide. It takes a heroic and talented waiter to stagger in with it." Weber seemed already to be already envisioning it as his eyes gleamed. "Also the price is fixed so you can eat as much of it as you want."

"Let's go for that," enthused Maxwell.

"It's too cold for beer," complained Rafferty.

"Then let's have red wine. Red isn't served chilled." Weber turned to Maxwell. "And you?"

"A Velvet, my good man," he said to the waiter. The waiter didn't even blink at this strange request. A good bartender never allowed himself to be caught unawares, as Maxwell well knew.

Both detectives were mystified and demanded to know what a Velvet was, especially since they were going to pay for it. "It's half and half of porter and champagne. It's got a great recoil."

"We'll stick to our wine. And while we're waiting, just what sort of information do you have for us?"

"It's about the Everleigh Club. Did you know Boylan was a regular?"

"You'd better have more than that. We've already there been on interviews. Don't tell me you frequent the club."

"Of course not. Say those two are really something. Did you know that every afternoon, leastwises when the weather permits, they go for a carriage drive with a coachman in livery and a team of black horses. They are accompanied each day by one of their beautiful girls, a different one each day, mind you. They've got on their best togs, silk and satin. They go to the bank to make their day's deposit. Now that's advertising.

"But nah, the Club's too rich for my blood. Still, us reporters have useful informants anxious for their moment of fame. If I can use what they give me, why then I might mention them favorably in some article or other." They were interrupted by the arrival of their platter of cold cuts and their drinks. The waiter was indeed staggering, preceded by a young lad who opened a folding table for the tray. After depositing the food, they then both bowed with a flourish in the direction of the smiling trio.

Nothing was heard about the Everleigh Club for some time as the men dug in into their repast. Weber was frequently called upon to tell them what they were eating. He had immediately forked liverwurst onto his own plate as it was a favorite. Sighs of happiness went around the table.

Finally, much later, during what was for Maxwell a breather, the conversation resumed. "There was this brouhaha, and a right strong one, between Boylan and another fellow at the Club."

"Now why didn't someone at the Club mention this to the two of us? "said an aggrieved Rafferty.

"And why am I not surprised?" Maxwell laughed. "Hey, those ladies know when discretion is needed. The other fellow is still alive and kicking and is good for plenty more visits. And he's got a full purse."

"And who is he?"

"Get this-it's Calvin Cordell of Commonwealth Edison." There was no reaction from Weber and Rafferty. "Don't you know about Cordell? Geez, you two aren't up on the big wheels in the business community if you've never heard of him."

"Then enlighten us," demanded Rafferty.

"It's all about franchises in Chicago." Rafferty's expression continued to be blank, though Weber nodded. "I'll have to explain the whole thing, and for that, I'll need another Velvet."

The waiter was immediately summoned so Maxwell could get on with his information.

"There's about thirty electric companies operating in Chicago, all competing for business and full capacity has grown to 3,200 kilowatts. Next year is the Columbian Exposition and a lot more electricity is going to be needed. Cordell is a Chief Executive Officer. And that's what caused the discord between Boylan and Cordell. Boylan did not like to see these companies demanding franchises and not even guaranteeing an improvement in service or lower prices. Boylan did not like their blackmailing demands nor did he approve of the same from the public transportation overlords. Yeah, I know Yerkes was at the wake, but he and Boylan were not chums, believe me. Anyway Cordell and Boylan had a rather sharp argument."

"For God's sake this Cordell certainly wouldn't do in Boylan," insisted Weber. "He's a businessman." Both Maxwell and Rafferty snickered at his whitewash of the business community. He gave them a look of chagrin.

"I keep thinking of that King Henry and Thomas Becket", declared Maxwell. "See the king, he says to his pals. 'That Becket's a pain in the ass,' and that was that."

"Too far-fetched." Weber and Rafferty did exchange looks. "However," said Rafferty, "there may well have been a disgruntled rival in the Levee. We'll have to think that over."

"As a postscript, there's a new guy on the block. Chicago Edison is going to have a new president. There's going to be consolidation. Cordell is going to be taking orders from Samuel Insull any day now."

"You need to give us a bit more for your supper."

"At your service, Charlie."

"Karl."

"Sorry, Karl. Anyway, I mentioned Boylan at the Everleigh Club." The two sergeants nodded. "Well, in Boylan's recent past, pre-Everleigh Club, he didn't frequent other bordellos. Your pal, the Alderman, preferred actresses. I'll bet the McCarthy boys had him shadowed; they would have known him to frequent stage doors not bordellos. He could have set up one or the other of these girls at a place of her own. But maybe they got to be too high maintenance 'cause he started going to the Everleigh Club. . . and that's where he finished. You understand I heard this all secondhand. The only place you can get the information is from the detective the McCarthys hired. You know, they'll claim they were protecting their sister, but

all that snooping meant they were just
aggravating themselves."

"I guess you've earned your lunch at least,"
said Rafferty.

Maxwell immediately called over their
waiter.

"My good man, I have a dog. I hope it won't
be too much trouble for you to put the leftovers
in a bag for him. Oh, and skip the liver sausage;
he doesn't like It." The waiter bowed and agreed
that no difficulty was caused by the request.

"Jaysus, Maxwell, have you even got a dog
much less one who sneers at liver sausage."

"I do not have a dog. However, we reporters
are not owner-managers or editors and . . .
leftovers is leftovers. After all, you've already
paid. Why waste it?" Both men had to laugh and
as he left with his bulging dog bag, waved
goodbye, and called after him, "When you get
more info, get in touch."

"What's next, Karl?"

"Back to the Club to find out what else the
sisters forget to tell us and why." At the Club,
they tried to impart a firmer tone to their
inquiries and also convoy disappointment at
having been denied vital information.

Minna Everleigh dismissed any allegation of
having failed to pass along anything of
significance.

"Whoever has come forward with that
information is mistaken. Yes, voices were risen
for a brief instant, but both parties were soon
directed away from one another by friends, so

the whole matter came to nothing. Boylan was our good patron and friend. We would do nothing to impede the investigation into his death. And Mr. Cornell is also a trusted patron and a man of prominence in the business world. He would never have dreamed of harming Alderman Boylan." She smiled. "So there you have it, gentlemen. Is there anything else with which I can help you?"

Rafferty and Weber put a good face on it and left.

"That was a big to-do over nothing. Not that I entirely believe her. But we can only pry out of her what she's willing to give. Maybe the next time we pay a visit, she might make more of an effort to disclose anything that'll help us with Boylan," Rafferty suggested. The two men decided to call it a day.

Weber called out, "Don't forget, plan on dinner with us Sunday."

CHAPTER EIGHT

Karl stood examining the family's Christmas cards which covered tables around the room. Gretel, precariously perched on a chair, was tacking the overflow around the parlor door frame.

"Decking the halls I see."

"That's next. Hand me more cards, Karl."

"The family's made quite a haul," her brother commented, "but I see a few addressed to you as well." He leaned forward, examining them.

"Don't go reading anything into those. They're from members of my cycling club. You'll note that they all have Santa Claus on them."

"Ah, but this Santa is stuffing a heart into a Christmas stocking." Before Gretel could retort, their father entered the room.

"What's this I hear? You want to invite a colleague for Sunday dinner just before Christmas. You've never done that before. A

Michael Rafferty? An Irishman!"

Karl took umbrage immediately, "He didn't come over on a boat." Karl's voice rose sharply. "He was born here the same as me."

"Don't get hot and bothered. I've got nothing against the Irish as such. But . . . you've got to admit that some of the Irish politicians are not models of good behavior."

"But most Irish are," Karl retorted. "They've got priests, teachers, doctors, and even lawyers, same as the Germans. They're not all like Bathhouse John or Hinky Dink Kenna or---

"The family knows that. Don't get so aggravated. God, you can be touchy." His father reached out a hand to placate him, but Karl ignored it.

"I'm tired of the ragging I get from this family about being on the police force. Well, I don't want to sit in an office all day. I get to meet people: good and bad and definitely more colorful than someone who wants to initiate a lawsuit against their neighbor over a foot of property. Nor am I interested in looking down throats all day long. Medicine isn't all saving lives in some miraculous fashion. It sounds tedious in fact. Anyway, as you should know since you own a newspaper even though it's in German, the Chicago Police Department is forward looking. Police officials have come from other cities to find out about the patrol boxes we've introduced. And we use a new identification system adopted from the French, the Bertillon System. We've got a traffic division." Karl had begun counting out police department achievements on his fingers. "We offer career work for women in the station houses; we've got the first police matrons to help runaway girls, the sick, the wounded and lost children."

Gretel immediately began asking questions about women on the force.

"Karl, tell her no. Or we'll have to contend with that as well."

"Father's right. "They want mature women experienced in dealing with these matters in their own lives." Having dismissed Gretel's inquiries, Karl turned back to his father. "Besides Rafferty and I have a lot in common. He's educated, reads a lot and is perfectly presentable. He attended prep the same as I did, though he was a few years ahead. He didn't go on to college. Maybe the costs were too high for his aunt and uncle."

"You should have finished and gotten your degree from St. Ignatius. That was a disappointment."

"I wasn't interested in the Classics."

"Classics build---"

"Character," finished Gretel as she climbed from the chair. "End the spat and hug." She pushed the two men together. They pulled her into the embrace.

Karl calmed down, looking a bit sheepish as well. "I knew you'd be agreeable so I've already invited Mike."

"So you knew your papa was an amiable old soul all along."

A few days later, the Sunday before

Christmas, the promised dinner finally took place. Karl borrowed his brother's buggy to pick Mike up in the early afternoon, the plan being that he was also to stay over. After protesting and being reassured that there was truly plenty of room, Mike finally agreed. His Aunt Maggie had been delighted, especially when she found out that the Webers were a Catholic family. It had been decided that the morning after the party, the two men would be driven part of the way downtown and would then manage getting to city hall using public transportation.

Before they arrived, Karl commented, "You look different; it's the clothes."

"The clerks at Field's did what they could. Aunt Maggie said that it was about time I took an interest in my appearance." So it was a very presentable Rafferty who was introduced to the Weber clan.

Before entering the multi-storied frame house, Mike took a moment to admire the veranda that wrapped itself almost completely around the house and the elegant landscaping as well. And there was the tall Christmas tree in the bay windows. It was all quite welcoming. He commented especially on the landscaping. His aunt had almost no lawn and barely any plantings at all.

"My mother enjoys that and supervises the folks we have coming in to do the work," Karl told him.

It was immediately obvious to Mike that the women of the household were keenly interested in him. Maybe having never met a Celt up close, and moreover such a close colleague's of Karl's, he was of more than unusual interest. His red hair and blue eyes were exactly what they'd imagined. Gretel found him quite good-looking and her intense scrutiny made him blush.

The whole family was in attendance, grandchildren included, so it was some time before--- coats discarded, scarves unwound, and introductions made--- everyone could relax in the parlor where the Christmas tree and a nativity scene were displayed, all of it creating a friendly ambiance. In a short time, the adults had all been served with wine which mellowed them still further.

The first toast officially welcomed Mike to the Weber home.

"We're glad finally to meet you. We've heard a lot about the adventures the two of you have had." Unfortunately, what immediately popped into Mike's mind was the Everleigh Club and he blushed again. He scrambled around searching for something he could say.

"We, that is my aunt and I, put up our first Christmas tree this year. You've got your candles lit; I'm afraid we've been a bit timid about that. They're on the tree, but we've been reluctant to light them."

"We're alert to the fact they can be a hazard," said Gretel, "so we keep a bucket of sand near the tree."

Mike laughed, "I'm reassured. Anyway, Germans have brought us a good many things that give the season more warmth." He pointed to the Christmas cards around the room. "Those as well. I see Santa Claus predominates."

"Thanks to Nast, Santa's sort of taken over," Karl agreed. At this point, conversation became more general, though Gretel monopolized Mike, asking him one question after another until they were finally called to dinner.

"A German dinner: roast pork, red cabbage, mashed potatoes, and more," announced Gretel. "On Christmas Day we'll have roast goose, at least, that's our tradition. What will your aunt make?"

"Turkey and all the trimmings probably. Same as Thanksgiving." Mike found a heaping plate in front of him. As the guest of honor, he'd been served first, but the others dug in quickly enough, and, for the time being, everyone concentrated on their food and wine. Karl turned to his brother-in-law with a query on Commonwealth Edison and Samuel Insull.

Mike meanwhile leaned over to Gretel, who sat on his right. "This is great stuff."

"I helped with the cooking." She was enjoying his company. He asked about her interests, and she was happy to oblige, putting in a bit of salesmanship about the merits of cycling. "Really, it's healthy fun-the exercise you know. Physicians endorse cycling. And the pneumatic tires today make it much easier."

Mike listened with an attempt at interest, but exercise, in fact, anything to do with sport except as an observer, was something of a foreign concept. He tried to imagine Gretel zipping all over Chicago on her bicycle and conjured up a quite a pretty picture.

From her other side, Karl, who'd finished
with his business inquiry and had begun listening
to Gretel's conversation, added, "She and her
club like cycling in Lincoln Park. It's not too
strenuous, Mike. You could rent a bike for a
nominal fee. . . ten cents." He laughed knowing
Mike's habits rather better than his sister did. He
also noted their seeming interest in one another.
Giving it further thought, Karl gave a faint shake
of the head. *No that won't do at all. He's older.
Nor* could he see his sister settled in the Irish
community, recent legacy or not.

"Karl doesn't cycle either," said his sister as
an afterthought. She said it with some scorn.
Then, the skirmish over cycling ended because
plates were being removed and dessert and coffee
handed around. Black Forest cake, Linzer Torte.
Desserts were not neglected by the Germans.
Finally, when everyone had their fill, a
suggestion was made for a bit of singing-
Christmas carols, of course. It seemed that with a
professor of music as head of the family, the
entire family was able to take a turn at the piano.

The sing-along ended with a rousing "Good
King Wenceslas," Karl adding his baritone and
Rafferty, a quite passable tenor. The evening
wound up, therefore, on a pleasant note before
they all retired to bed. It seemed that some of the
family lived in their own homes not far away, so
that indeed, there was plenty of room for Mike.

The following morning had involved the
cooks in a bit of serious pre-party discussion over
Mike's breakfast. It was the usual practice to
have just rolls and coffee, but Mike might need a

heavier breakfast of bacon, eggs, toast, tomatoes. and God knows what else to keep him going.

"You know, "said Gretel, "my friend Louisa's family has broiled mackerel with baked potatoes, or lamb hash and cracked wheat."

Her mother frowned; it didn't sound too tasteful to her. " But if Michael is the only one who eats that much, he might feel he's inconveniencing us." They finally opted for rolls and coffee, and he seemed perfectly satisfied.

The two detectives were dropped off as planned to catch a street car to City Hall, wondering at their own optimism at using public transportation. It was still damned cold; the policeman on the corner was beating his hands together and stamping his feet in order to keep warm.

"I hope the heater on the street car is working. I'm half frozen already," complained Karl.

"And I hope the fookin' car isn't running late."

"No, I see it coming. But, damn, it's stuffed with Christmas shoppers. They won't be getting off here. We'll just have to cram in the best we can. I'm not waiting for the next one." And they did manage, hanging on to rails and straps for dear life. Getting out near city hall, they ended up joining a jam of holiday shoppers on the sidewalk. Traditional Christmas songs could be heard coming from many of the big stores. Folks were stopping to view the delights offered in the display windows.

The red kettles of the Salvation Army reappeared on the street as well, the bell-ringing accompaniment making an additional happy sound.

"They must have done pretty well last year to stage a repeat performance. It may be the start of a tradition," commented Karl. Besides the shoppers, there were also peddlers on the sidewalk hawking cheap toys from push-carts and further impeding the pedestrians.

"Where are the cops who usually move these fellows along?"

"It's Christmas, and they're filled with the milk of human kindness," retorted Mike. Giving the matter more thought, he added, "These fellas get hustled all the rest of the year as it is." They passed one woman, with a worn shawl bargaining with a peddler for a bear on a stick and a bit of glittery ribbon.

Karl pointed out poorly-clad youngsters, flattening their noses against the cold glass of shop windows filled with toys.

"Fat chance those little girls have of getting one of those fancy dolls or the boys in getting a train," he said. It made him momentarily sad, but the carols soon put him back into the Christmas spirit.

The men finally reached city hall and entered a lobby redolent with the smell of balsam and pine from boughs and a large Christmas tree. There was even a trio of carolers doing the old standards.

"That's sure an improvement over the usual smell of cigars, and the odor left from the bums sleeping in the lobby last night." Karl winked at his partner.

The greenery continued up the staircase and even the detective bureau had its share. Quite a stir was going on and Steele came out of his office with a, "Thank goodness you two have arrived. We're leaving right now in the police van. There's been another murder." He pushed them out the door, and they hurried in his wake along with Willie until they reached the van.

After that, the clanging bell insured as swift a drive as possible to Boylan's saloon.

"It's Plotz," announced Rafferty as soon as the men were seated.

"And how did you know that?"demanded Steele.

"I just thought she was holdin' something back. I couldn't get her to cough up though. She really was in a good place to have had a listen even if she denied it."

At the saloon, uniformed police showed them to the kitchen.

"It's here a barkeep found her this morning, head bashed in." McCarthy stood in front of the open door to the kitchen wringing his hands. "What a disaster! What next? You men have to clear this up."

"Has the coroner been here yet?" Steele asked one of the uniformed policemen.

"He's on his way." There was a commotion in the hall and the coroner appeared.

"Where's the body?" he demanded. Steele took his arm and escorted him into the kitchen.

Everyone else continued to hover in the hallway.

Weber motioned McCarthy aside. "Why don't you go back into the saloon. When we know anything, I'll personally clue you in." McCarthy nodded, and left still wringing his hands and murmuring about the recent dire events.

Everyone else continued to stand in the hallway until they were finally rewarded by the coroner declaring Mrs. Plotz dead.

"Someone bashed in the front of her head, no doubt with that cast iron frying pan on the floor. It has blood on it. By the way, rigor has come and gone." He pried open her right hand. "There, I thought she was clutching something. I could see a bit of paper sticking out." He held out his find. "It's part of a bill. Can't tell the denomination. She might have been holding a lot more, hanging on tightly and the killer overlooked this bit."

"So she was facing her killer?" asked Steele.

"I would say so. The attack must have come as a surprise."

"She was for sure trying to blackmail somebody, the fool woman," declared Rafferty. He looked at the body, pathetic now in its old firmly-belted robe and wearing a pair of worn slippers. But Mrs. Plotz's kitchen was immaculate, table scrubbed down, sink and oven glistening. "Ah, shite, she had a chance to give us Boylan's killer. Instead she tried blackmail."

"With McCarthy losing business and cutting back, she probably thought she'd be out on the street and so she resorted to blackmail." But Weber too shook his head at the woman's foolishness.

Steele motioned to Weber and Rafferty.

"You two go and question McCarthy. I want to know how in the hell a murderer comes and goes as he pleases. The buildings next door belonged to Boylan as well. They're empty now. Doesn't McCarthy know how to lock doors!"

McCarthy insisted that, yes, he had locked the doors between the buildings. "There's no gambling now. We put a stop to all that. I'm trying to rent or sell the places as a hotel or rooming house. I certainly don't want a gaming establishment or house of ill repute next door."

"But did you lock the doors between the buildings?"asked Rafferty. "That's most likely where the murderer came from for both murders. He certainly wouldn't have risked going through the saloon."

"Of course we made sure any egress to the next building was not possible ."

"And did entail putting on new locks?"

"No. Oh dear. I guess that means someone else has keys," he said his voice full of chagrin. "And the key holder could come and go as he pleased." His tone changed, "We'll change that damned omission today." He called Sloan. "Send out someone to get a locksmith pronto."

"Lockin' the barn door after the horse's gotten out," snorted Rafferty.

While Weber continued to commiserate with McCarthy, Rafferty looked around the saloon and once more noted the large painting of Custer's Last Stand. The evening his illness had taken hold, it had seemed a marvelous and heroic battle, now it just looked like a dismal defeat.

Soothingly, Weber said, "Mr. McCarthy, at least the egress problem will finally be taken care of, though the murderer probably has no further reason to use that particular entrance." Then leaving McCarthy to his woes, the two men rejoined Steele and reported their latest information. The coroner and the body were both in the process of departing. Steele was looking through the cook's meager possessions.

"Nothing much here. No message saying so-and-so is responsible if you find my corpse." He looked at his two detectives. "Track down who's got keys. Get a hold of that Duffy and Fitzpatrick. They'd know, probably got keys themselves. I've need to try and track down any kin of Mrs. Plotz. You interview the employees here. I still have more of her property to poke through." He pointed to the room off the kitchen she'd used as her bedroom.

Rafferty and Weber reentered the saloon. "Mr. McCarthy who had keys to those back doors?

"As far as I know, only myself and Sloan, and he's turned his in. I've got Boylan's set."

"Did the cook have a set?"

"Certainly not."

"If you can think of anything else relative to the latest murder, please contact our headquarters at once." McCarthy nodded to Weber; Rafferty he ignored.

Consulting his partner, Weber asked, "It's still early. Want to tackle Duffy and Fitzpatrick since they're not far away?" But Rafferty stopped Weber before he had a chance to move on.

"Who in the hell would Plotz consider harmless enough to ask for the money face to face. For sure she would have gone a more roundabout way with someone definitely villainous. Let's think about that. Or maybe that's not how the whole scene played out. Ah, who knows exactly what went on. Karl, I'd really rather interview staff here about Plotz before we go chasing down Duffy and Fitzpatrick. I'll ask Steele if we can start here."

"Suits me." Steele was only too happy to finish with the crime scene and return to headquarters. He hadn't found anything to aid him in tracking down any kin.

Returning to the saloon, Weber asked, "Mr. McCarthy, we'd like to interview your staff regarding Mrs. Plotz."

He agreed at once. No more angry bluster. He seemed defeated and announced he was going home for the day.

"I've had enough. Sloan's in charge; ask anyone here anything. And Sloan," he called across the room, "get in some food for the free lunch. Direct the locksmith. If you really need me, send word around."

Sloan joined the two detectives at a table, leaving someone else to tend the bar which had more customers than usual.

"Yeah, business is up. Looky-loos wanting to know about the murder. At least they're drinking." He sighed. "Business hasn't been too good since Boylan passed." He looked sincerely saddened by the catastrophe that had struck what he considered his saloon. "So how can I help you?"

Rafferty took the lead.

"We need whatever you can tell us about Plotz. Did she have visitors? Did she go out visitin'? I mean what did she do when she wasn't tendin' the kitchen?"

Sloan ordered them all a brew.

"She was a loner. She did not have visitors, and she only left the premises to go to the wholesalers who provide the victuals. And I guess she went to some church cause she went out every Sunday morning at the same time. Otherwise she kept herself to herself. Say, Henry might know a bit more. He's another one of Boylan's charities like Plotzy and Fitzpatrick. You know about Fitzpatrick?"

"We heard about him from the ladies at the Everleigh Club."

"Yeah, the ladies at the sportin' clubs have a soft spot for him. Good-lookin' kid. Well, Plotzy was a charity of Boylan's as well. A poor widow he heard about, so he took her on. Henry is another such charity. Badly hurt at the stable where he was working. He's lame. But he's great at cleaning up here. He's the reason the brass rail is kept to a real shine. He dosses down in one of the storerooms. You know, a cot, food etc. Whenever Mrs. Plotz went out shopping, he accompanied her.

"Hey Henry! Come over here. These two detectives need some info on Mrs. Plotz."

An elderly man limped over. "Yeah, real shame about her. Not that we was buddies." Rafferty pointed to a chair, inviting him to join them and Sloan ordered him a beer.

"Wotcha want to know?"

"She have any visitors, Henry?" Weber began the questioning.

"Heck no. She was a real loner. Stuck to her kitchen. Read her German newspapers and books too if she could get a hold of 'em. I sat with her for a time or two havin' coffee, but she really wasn't good company. Always complainin' she was, about our clientele, about the Republicans and the Demycrats and jest about everything else. So I left her to it. And on our trips to the wholesalers, well, that was just once in a while cuz mostly with the orders, there wasn't much of a change from one time to the next. And we didn't have to lug the stuff back. It was delivered."

"What about her Sunday church?"

"That was to one of those storefront missions, and I don't think she hung around." He scratched his head. "Maybe it was hard for her, being a German and all, in an Irish saloon. But she didn't try goin' anywheres else."

Sloan motioned him back to work.

Rafferty groaned. "That didn't get us anywhere. I don't see how anyone in her life could have caused her death, so it's got to be because of Boylan." He looked around the room." Say Sloan, where's your piano player? He gave the place some class. We could interview him as well."

"He beat it when McCarthy came on board. Heard him talking about cutting and trimming and generally ranting all over the place and just lit out. McCarthy ain't replaced him."

"Oh . . . and we heard you had a key to the building next door."

"And I give it to McCarthy." He smirked. "Duffy and Fitzpatrick had keys, and so did the managers of the other side of our little organization, you know next door." Sloan still seemed reluctant to mention the gambling. Rafferty groaned at the additional questioning this would entail.

Weber rose. "Thanks for the information.

Sloan commiserated with the two men then went back to the bar.

"So it's on to Duffy and Fitzpatrick. Maybe they know about the managers and their keys. This whole thing is getting out of hand. Damn it, there's keys all over the place." The two men again made their way to the hotel where the two bodyguards had been residing and where they were presumably still in residence.

"Oh, it's youse again. They're in the same place you saw them the last time, our most elegant parlor," the desk clerk snickered.

And they were there, presumably not having found employment elsewhere - Duffy playing solitaire and Fitzpatrick restlessly pacing up and down.

"What is it this time?"inquired Duffy, throwing down the cards.

"We've some news and some questions," declared Rafferty. He addressed Duffy but kept his eyes on Kevin. "It's a question of keys. And a question about another murder. It seems Mrs. Plotz was done in last night." Fitzpatrick remained expressionless except for a widening of the eyes; Duffy's mouth dropped open.

"It seems as if someone with keys had a way to get to the kitchen and brained Mrs. Plotz."

"Geez, why would anyone want to do that?"

"Well, Duffy me lad, to keep a secret, secret. It seems the old lady may have seen or heard more than was good for her. And, it appears, she expected someone to pay." Still, focused on Fitzpatrick, Rafferty finally saw some kind of emotion though what that stifled gasp meant if anything, who knew? He shrugged. He'd have to give it further thought that was for sure.

Weber now demanded information on keys, who had them and when. "Who used the door between the buildings." After a few moments without a response, he demanded, "Well what about it? We want answers."

"Geez, we've still got ours. McCarthy didn't ask for them, and we weren't goin' to volunteer that information or anythin' else to that shite."

"Produce them," demanded Rafferty. Duffy reached into his pants pocket, took out a set of keys, extracted one and tossed it over.

"And yours?" he asked Fitzpatrick. Kevin did the same, removing one from the ring and handing it to Rafferty.

"Have you been using your keys?" demanded Weber.

"Of course not, no reason to. Remember, McCarthy cut us off." Fitzpatrick sat down. He looked rather like the stuffing had been knocked out of him.

"Have you been in touch with Mrs. Plotz for any reason since the murder of Boylan."

"No, no reason. Even if we communicated with her before, it was only ever on some errand for Boylan. An order for hot soup and a hot toddy for instance," said Fitzpatrick staring at Rafferty, definitely reminding him of that night when he'd had to trot along to the kitchen to get something nourishing for Rafferty. It seemed to Mike as if he still resented it. Were they some kind of rivals?

"What about the managers of the gambling rooms next door? We heard they had keys." Duffy nodded.

"Don't know what's happened to those. Guys were fired by McCarthy when he closed up that part of the business. Maybe they turned their keys in to him." They hadn't and now they'd have to track those down as well.

"Let's let Willie track those down," said Weber and Rafferty nodded. He'd grown sick of the game of who's got the keys.

"Listen, you two, if you can think of anyone Plotz could have blackmailed, or anything at all that could help us solve her murder, contact us. You hear?" With that demand, Weber motioned Rafferty back to the lobby.

"Now what? Back to headquarters?"

"I guess. Say, Karl, really let's go somewhere, have a glass of somethin' and think about the old lady's murder. I still can't get over her actually being face to face with someone she's demanding money from, I mean, if that's the way it played out. Let's let Steele give it a think too. And he can have the keys, they're useless now anyway."

Later, at headquarters, all three agreed that Duffy and Fitzpatrick could have had a way in that would have allowed them to commit both murders, but couldn't really see them as the guilty parties.

CHAPTER NINE

On arriving at headquarters the following day, hoping to see Steele for further instructions, Karl and Mike were greeted at his door by none other than the ebullient Bathhouse John Coughlin who immediately informed them he knew the culprit they sought.

"Mr. Coughlin here may have cracked the case. He knows of an old enemy in the Levee," said Steele.

"No maybes about it. Got the fella. Jest told your boss. Patrick Boylan was a saint, a saint, I say. He never could stomach some of these out and out scoundrels and wanted them gone from the Levee. The man in question, detectives, is Frank Fergus McMurtry. A dastardly fellow if there ever was one. Course he'll have an alibi. Plenty of filthy crooks will swear he was with them dolin' out soup to the needy. That'll be the day. Break 'em down. Get McMurtry in here.

You'll see that's the man what shot my good friend Boylan. Rogue would do it himself too. Up to all sorts of evil doin's."

"Mr. Coughlin," said Steele holding out his hand, "you can be sure we'll be looking into this. Thank you for the tip-off."

"I'm goin' now and write a poem in honor of me old pal Boylan. He deserves it. In fact, I'm inspired right now, fellas. He took what he must have regarded as an oratorical stance and, to the astonishment of the others, began. "'In all the years Boylan served as a member of the First, he never took a crooked dime, nor even a weinerwurst. He heard a lot of foolish talk regarding 'easy mon'. But Boylan I will defend from slander's flippant tongue.'" And with a final wave of his hand and a last flash of his striped Prince Albert coat, plaid vest and pants, he headed out.

The three men stared after his vanishing figure. "A poem indeed," declared Rafferty. "Still, it's somewhat more than eloquent than his 'She Sleeps at the Side of the Drainage Canal'?"

"Do I detect some sarcasm, Mike?"

"The likes of Bathhouse John gets connected to the Irish community and that is not what we're all about. It aggravates me when folks do that and you know it. God, Bathhouse John is not a boutonniere in the dress coat of an Irish gentleman."

Both Weber and Steele laughed at Rafferty's attempt at a witticism. The lieutenant added seriously, "Well, boys, guess who's going to visit McMurtry?"

"But what in blazes could he have to do with the murder of Mrs. Plotz? The two murders have to be tied together."

"I agree and yet-who knows? Maybe Mrs. Plotz knew other secrets she thought she could cash in on. You have to admit that's a possibility. In the meantime, follow up Coughlin's lead. Bathhouse John's too important to ignore. You know he'll be the next alderman. I've heard that the Democratic Committee has already made its decision."

"Yeah, and they've already decided how to divide the boodle," said Weber, laughing.

"Stop smirking, Karl, the Germans produce some questionable politicos themselves."

"At least ours don't produce dubious poetry."

"You two stop your blathering and go see if this McMurtry leads to something worthwhile." The lieutenant waved them away.

Once out of the office, Rafferty groaned, "Jaysus, do you know what part of the Levee we've got to visit to find Frank Fergus? We'll need bodyguards ourselves." He suddenly looked like he had a eureka moment. "Speaking of bodyguards. Let's go get us a couple."

Back at the rooming house, the clerk grinned even more.

"Say, you two are back again. As it turns out we do have a couple of vacant rooms if youse want to stay on a more permanent basis. I can give a good weekly rate."

"Just tell us if Duffy and Fitzpatrick are still

around." Weber gave him a disgruntled look.

"Same old place." The clerk pointed in the direction of the same parlor.

"Ah, shite, they're back again. What now?" demanded Duffy.

"We need a couple of bodyguards who are willing to work for nothing. We need your Levee expertise. We're still on Boylan's case and have a new clue. . . delivered in person by Bathhouse John Coughlin. And you two will be the experts on this subject. It seems Frank Fergus McMurtry has been fingered as the murderer by Coughlin, and we have to find him and question him."

Duffy and Fitzpatrick started laughing. "Fat chance of that."

"That's why you two will be with us."

"We're not crazy."

"Do you two want to keep staying here rent free? We can notify McCarthy that his brother-in-law has a nice property here, and we're sure he'll be as pleased as punch to inspect the premises."

"That's blackmail, that is," wailed Duffy. Weber and Rafferty sat down and let the two bodyguards mull it over. They even retreated into a corner of the room to discuss the matter and finally agreed, "We ain't got no choice."

Half an hour later, the four men reached Whiskey Row, the west side of State Street from Van Buren to Harrison, where every building was occupied by a saloon, a wine-room with girls, a gambling-house, or all three thrown together.

Here were the worst dives, harboring thieves and pickpockets, one of whom was a Johnny Rafferty. Mike frequently and indignantly had to deny any kinship with this notorious thief.

"Well," asked Duffy, "who do you want to ask about Frank Fergus? Mushmouth Johnson maybe or Johnny Rafferty, Tom McGinnis, Sime Tuckhorn. Mind you, the two of us do not have a speaking acquaintance with any of these fellas. All's we know is their names and reputations. I mean, Boylan didn't socialize with the likes of them."

"What about Al Connolly? He's the Democratic Committeeman for the First Ward-not that being the Democratic Committeeman is any guarantee of honesty. But he's more presentable at least," offered Fitzpatrick.

"Lead the way," said Weber encouragingly. Duffy and Fitzpatrick leading the way, the four men entered Connolly's saloon, a new place, opened just the year before and not yet showing the wear and tear of some of the older establishments.

"Will you look at that. There's a Christmas wreath over the bar and swags of holly around the room. He's actually celebrating the season," declared Weber with wonder.

They were lucky, because Connolly was on the premises. He even recognized Duffy and waved him over.

"Lookin' for a new job, Brian? I thought after workin' for Boylan you'd be too upstanding to come around here."

"Nah, we've been forced into helping the

cops in their inquiry."

Connolly closely scrutinized the rest of Duffy's party.

"So what brings you fellas here? It ain't Party business that I know."

Weber spoke up, "Bathhouse John fingered Frank Fergus McMurtry for the murder of Boylan and we're trying to track him down. We know he doesn't have a place of own. We heard he and his cronies operate out of a number of places."

"Bathhouse John ought to keep his yap shut. The showoff. He wants to be Mr. Clean now he's getting up in the political world. Boylan wasn't murdered by anyone on Whiskey Row. He didn't like us particularly, but he left us alone and we left him alone. Anyway, he had a gamblin' den of his own, so he wasn't all that saintly. I got to admit I kind of admired him. He got himself rich and richer with more than gamblin'. He was into property, nice properties and investments, the kind of stuff Yerkes and Field and dem holier than thou types play around with. Me, I find that stuff confusin'. I'm goin' to stick to fixing and bein' a bondsman."

He laughed at the indignation on Rafferty's face.

"You're pal," he said to Weber, "is taking up the cudgels for the good Irish I see."

"About McMurtry, Mr. Connolly," Weber insisted.

"I ain't seen him for a week or more. I don't know where he's holed up now and I don't particularly want to know either. He's never been the flavor of the month around here."

"Any idea where we should go next."

Connolly shrugged. "Nah, he's tough, always fightin'. Can't stay in one place long enough. Why Bathhouse John fingered him, I don't know. Unless, he wants to show how law-abiding he is now that he's movin' on to the city council chambers. What next? At least their meetings will be a whole lot more colorful. There ain't anyone more colorful than old Bathhouse John."

"Thanks for giving us some time, and by the way, nice decorations." With that, Weber took his party back to the door.

"No trouble," Connolly called to their retreating backs.

On the street, Rafferty said, "We're not going to get anywhere wandering up and down Whiskey Row. In my book, the McMurtry tip is all shite anyway. He turned to Duffy and Fitzpatrick.

"As far as I'm concerned, you two can go back to your hotel, and we promise not to tell McCarthy about the location. But he'll know soon enough. The family lawyer is searching through the records trying to pin down all of Boylan's properties."

After they left Whiskey Row, all four of them with relief, Weber and Rafferty took off for headquarters having decided in advance to tell Steele that their efforts had not and would not bare any fruit. And if that didn't suit Bathhouse John, why then let him find McMurtry's location and they'd of course declare themselves grateful.

"But I bet that's the last we'll hear of it. Like Connolly said, he just wants to be a Mr. Clean now that he's headin' for the City Council."

At City Hall, Steele agreed with Rafferty and Weber. Rafferty suggested he and Weber could go and interview the private dick the McCarthy family had hired.

"Of course, our pal McCarthy probably has to ease us in there. I'm sure he will, but tomorrow will have to do. McCarthy's probably at home right now with an ice bag on his head." He laughed. "Wait until he hears Bathhouse John is goin' to be the new alderman."

"Plus," added Weber, "Carter Harrison has a good chance of being the next mayor, and his stance on saloons and their activities is not going to sit well with McCarthy."

That is just what they heard the next day: lamentations, acute distress, and a declaration that the family had had all they could take after Weber gave him the ward's future political prognosis. Not just the building next door but the saloon as well were going to be sold, declared the beleaguered McCarthy.

"You're selling in a good market. It should get snapped up. The Levee will be doing excellent business during the Fair and this is one of the better locations and properties."

"I only hope we get rid of it quickly."

"Maybe you could stipulate that the new owners should keep on old Henry. That would be a real act of Christian charity," added Rafferty.

"You're right. Yes, I will stipulate that. The old gentleman is a hard worker." McCarthy looked pleased with himself.

In an aside to Rafferty, Weber continued, "While we're here, let's get the name of the detective agency before McCarthy vanishes. And we can only hope that bears some fruit."

Mike gave a snort. He was getting essimistic about their whole inquiry.

"This case is getting too complicated. There's enough red herrings, and I'm sure that's what they probably are. . . to sink a ship. This case needs more than the likes of us. It needs that new fella, that Sherlock Holmes, or Arsene Lupin. We're also havin' to run every suspect by Duffy and Fitzpatrick, and I'm getting tired of chasing the two of them down. Ah, go and get the name of that private detective and a letter from McCarthy giving us permission to pry into the family's inquiries.

After an initial surprise that they even knew about the detective, McCarthy had no problem admitting that the family had hired someone to trail Boylan.

"We're the ones who looked out for our sister and niece." He also admitted that Boylan did seem to avoid bordellos and confined himself to a couple of actresses he had set up, one at a time. Shaking his finger at Rafferty and Weber, he lectured, "But that's still reprehensible for a married man." After a pause, he added, "Hang on a bit and I'll write that letter you want."

After their long day, including getting to Whiskey Row and back to Boylan's, the partners decided to delay visiting the detective agency -

which was in still another neighborhood and
meant further cable car trips - until the next day.

CHAPTER TEN

"That's a blessing for you, Mike, the office is only up one flight of stairs. And the building's fairly respectable. I was a little dubious knowing how the McCarthys are a mite careful with their pocketbook."

Rafferty took the lead and they were soon at the door of the office.

"Jaysus, Tinker's Detective Agency. Is he tryin' to horn in on the Pinkerton Agency's name and fame?"

"Mike, it may actually be the man's name. You're getting suspicious about everything. And to think Gretel called you charming and funny."

That brought up a smile.

"She really called me charming and funny?" He'd been about to open the door, when a sudden suspicion hit him. "Just when did she say that?"

"I'm not making it up, for God's sake. She told me Sunday evening when the folks were showing you your room. She took me aside." Karl put up his hands in a gesture of frustration. "Forget it. I'm sorry I said anything." And he began silently berating himself for carelessly dropping the remark. Mike, though, was again grinning from ear to ear, this time he finally opened the door.

Tinker's Agency was not a fly-by-night establishment. A male receptionist graced the outer office and there were several doors which led to other offices, showing that Tinker's had a number of agents in its employ.

The two sergeants stated their business. Upon consulting his files, the receptionist directed them to Tinker himself.

"You're in luck, he's in. But let me check if he can see you immediately."

A brief parley with Tinker made it clear the man was available and they were shown into his office.

"How may I help you, officers."

The man looked neither like a ferret or a hound. In fact, he had no unusual characteristics at all. *He must be good at tailing,* thought Karl.

Tinker's eyes opened wide when he heard they were investigating the murder of Alderman Boylan. Weber took the lead

"We know from the McCarthy family that they wanted information on Boylan's activities, especially the extra-marital ones. We've got a letter from them allowing us access to your files. Your clients are as anxious to have this murder solved as we are. If we can get the names of the ladies with whom Boylan was involved and can interview them, maybe . . . just maybe . . . they can clue us in on other aspects of his life. And perhaps some of the other activities you observed may help us still more." Weber handed over the letter.

After reading the letter, Tinker declared that he saw no problem. After a brief search in his filing cabinet, he pulled out the relevant material.

"If the McCarthys are happy to release the material, and, after all, Boylan is deceased, so here it is. You know, the Alderman didn't really sneak around. He was a very easy man to trail and on whom to gather data. After our initial contact and the establishment of a sort of pattern, we were told we need only keep a periodic eye on him to see if there were any changes. I can tell you now that from the time we began, there were no more than two liaisons, the first going on for some time. Why exactly he left one and went on to the other, I don't know. You'll have to ask the ladies, if you can find them. Then, later of course, he became a steady customer of the Everleigh Club.

"At that point, the McCarthys ceased their survey." He paused. "Good luck on your case. There's nothing that Boylan did that really made him reprehensible. The gambling they already knew about, so we stopped pursuing that. As for the boodle, well, the McCarthys suspected that too. I believe it was the lady friends they were really interested in. You know, having a mistress or two, well . . . that's hardly a reason for me to malign Boylan. Believe me, we've had to shadow much nastier parties."

Tinker suddenly chuckled then broke into a full-fledged laugh. After he could control himself again, he apologized.

"You know, and I never reported all the details of this incident to the McCarthys because it wasn't really relevant, but I've got to share it with someone." He chuckled again.

"It's to do with his last lady friend, one Lizette LaForce, who claimed to have worked with Eddie Foy himself which I rather doubt. You know we used to bribe the janitor of her apartment building, which by the way Boylan owned, for little tidbits like that. The young lady was left alone a lot of the time. I suspect the Alderman saw more of his saloon and even his wife than he did of Miss Lizette. According to the janitor, she sat alone most of the time and read, took her spaniel for strolls, enjoyed the company of her cleaning lady, and now and then hosted a few giggling girls probably from the same chorus line.

"At any rate, again according to the janitor, an insurance salesman came to her door. For lack of company, she invited him in. He returned on other occasions, and he certainly wasn't spending all that time selling her an insurance policy. Well, now comes the funny part.

"One day Boylan shows up and the janitor hightails it after him because it seems he has to pass on a letter from the lady friend. Boylan's in the apartment by this time. The place is now minus all the knickknacks, the occasional tables, and after a brief search, all the kitchen wares, linens, plus her books. She left the big stuff and three books: a dictionary, a speller, and the History of the Roman Empire. The note explained that she felt what was taken was owed to her. Boylan's reaction was to sit down on the sofa and start laughing. Sort of like me, first a grin, then a chuckle, then a hardy laugh.

"Now the janitor had noticed the insurance man and Lizette removing the articles, but she'd bribed him to cease noticing just as she'd paid him earlier not to mention the insurance man while the fellow was conducting his courtship. I didn't tell the McCarthys. It doesn't really put Boylan in a bad light so they probably wouldn't have been interested. Oh, and by the way, he'd already begun frequenting the Everleigh Club.

"Boylan also laughed about the three books. It seems he bought those to educate her. She only took her own books, which according to the janitor, all seemed to have screaming women running away from mansions and castles."

"Gothics," interjected Weber. "My sister reads them now and then."

"Gentlemen, let me get you the name and last known address of the first lady friend we observed and any previous information on Lizette. And good luck to you."

Once out in the hallway, the detectives talked over what they'd discovered.

"A lot of nothing", grumbled Mike.

"I think we cleared up any connection he had with the Clan na Gael. Well, maybe, but it does seem as if he's only ever tracked to meetings of Loyal Hibernians."

"More dead ends."

Mike moved over to a bench in the hallway and sat down.

"Hold on a minute. What's next? We need another plan. It ain't goin' to take long to track down his first lady friend if the address is current. In fact, let Willie do the huntin'. He's good and persistent, but if he does by some miracle find her, I'll bet she has as little info as Evangelina.

"Let's go to the address Tinker gave us and see the layout," suggested Karl. "Maybe we can track down the insurance salesman, if the janitor knows the name of his company." As it turned, out that was another fruitless journey and then both men were ready to call it quits for the day.

"That's it. Food and drink are called for. Care to join me."

"Jaysus, you sure like your meals punctual. How far do we have to go until you're satisfied with what's on offer?"

"It just so happens --"

"Do you know every good dining establishment in Chicago?"

"At least the German ones." And the two men were shortly seated in yet another pseudo-Rathskeller where Karl soon put in an order for young beef liver sauteed in bacon fat.

Mike ordered a schnitzel with which he was at least familiar and added a relaxing beer.

"Tell me again about your sister and how much she liked my company." Mike grinned. "Remember I don't get much attention from girls so your sister's comment was, well, awfully nice to hear."

"Listen Mike, anyone interested in our Gretel needs to take up cycling, ice skating, dancing and . . . not just the waltz. She likes a good ethnic twirl and stomp. Oh, and she also likes being rowed around the Lincoln Park lagoons. I've had to do it on occasion."

Mike looked appalled.

Karl started to laugh. "What a sight, the Weber family Amazon meets Inert Man."

"Damn it, I ain't inert."

"So what do you call sitting at prize fights and baseball games? Vigorous exercise?"

"The two of us get plenty of exercise walkin' and tryin' to track down miscreants each and every day." Mike's serious expression changed, and he grinned. "And chasin' cable cars in all kinds of weather. And anyway I played baseball."

"Ah, the past tense. Actually, our Gretel has more freedom than say, the daughter of a manual laborer or even in the average middle class family. Yes, my parents tolerate her activities, but they're grateful she isn't a suffragette yet. When she heard about how the Pinkerton Agency uses women, they call them Pink Roses, as detectives, she considered for a moment doing just that---needless to say my father and grandfather absolutely refused to give their approval to that particular idea."

"Well, I admire her. My aunt is a mighty independent lady herself, what with running her own business and doing charitable work in the Irish community besides. I can tell you, Karl, she fears God . . . but nothing else.

After a brief pause, Mike continued, "But it's time I got away from her apron strings."

"You don't appear dependent on your aunt."

"I didn't mean exactly that. Sure, I go my own way, but I live in her home. I try to be there for her, probably because she and my Uncle Frank raised me after my parents got the typhoid and died. It's getting difficult though. Look how far I have to travel to get home. It's closer to work I should be livin'. This would give me more

time for meself. Yet I do live rent-free," he
mused. At this point Karl rolled his eyes.

"There's plenty of rooming houses south of
the Loop stores and offices."

"They don't really appeal to me either.
Those clerks spendin' their whole lives livin' in a
roomin' house. Die there as well."

"This discussion is getting gloomy."

"Yeah, well, the weather doesn't help. Nor
the idea of going back home, waitin' for transport
and changin' transport, all in this cold. I leave in
the pitch dark and get back in the pitch dark."

"Don't you doss down with some of the
fellows that live closer in?"

"If I get word to them in time, they'll let me
use their sofas. Say, Karl, isn't there a pocket of
Irish livin' north of the river?"

"As a matter of fact, there is, though not in
the numbers like the back of the stockyards."

"I got to look into that."

"I wouldn't advise it. It's the poorer sort live
there. It's home to tanneries, not a salubrious
place at all. Steer clear."

"In the meantime. . . got any more practical
recommendations?"

"How about the hotel Fitzgerald and Duffy
are using. That's closer and it looks a decent
enough place."

Mike nodded, and at that point, both men
decided to change the subject.

"Look," said Mike, "tomorrow I want to get
back to Boylan's and see if there's anything more
to be learned from Plotz's things. If that is,
McCarthy hasn't cleared them out. I don't think

he has. He was too frazzled that last time we saw him."

"But now we have to report back to Steele, besides which we're also way behind in our paperwork. I'm going to headquarters. I'll even volunteer to begin the write-up. I'm tired of traipsing around pointlessly and running into nothing but dead ends. We need a new direction. If you can find one at Boylan's and need me call headquarters and I'll join you." So Karl and Mike agreed to split up at least until mid-afternoon. If there were no new leads, Mike would come back to City Hall. Then they could rethink what path they'd take and bring Steele in on it as well. "Meanwhile I'll send hound-dog Willie on his errand to track down Miss Lizette ."

On his way to Boylan's, Rafferty grumbled to himself that Christmas was only a few days away, and he hadn't had any time to enjoy its approach except for last Sunday's dinner with the Weber family. I ain't even had time to buy Aunt Maggie her gift. Deciding to take the time for gift hunting after his present effort to gain additional clues into Boylan's death, he strode into the saloon.

The only evidence of the season were a few wreaths placed here and there and, as usual, Sloan was behind the bar. The man must sleep around the corner . . . or back of the bar, thought Mike. Business seemed to be down again; the looky-loos had presumably found something else to be nosy about. Mrs. Plotz demise was no longer of any interest.

Sloan actually waved at Mike as if happy to

see hm.

"Come to visit us again? What's it this time?"

"I want to examine Mrs. Plotz's possessions, if they're still here, that is."

"No problem. No one has been into the room except to make coffee or to heat something up for ourselves instead of stickin' to the cold stuff in the free lunch."

Rafferty took the time to look around and was surprised to see Duffy sitting at a table and staring into his beer stein with a very long face indeed.

"I thought you weren't supposed to be here."

"I'm a paying customer. I'm not looking for a handout from McCarthy. Anyway, the big boss ain't here. Sit down, Sergeant Rafferty, and join me. I need someone to lend an ear, and you're better than most." Mike sat. "It's about Kevin. That's why I'm here. Couldn't take his pacing and mumbling anymore. He's always been a fella what keeps his thoughts to himself, but now that he's muttering and pacing enough to wear out the rug, why, it's worse than ever. Do you think he ought to see a doctor?"

"What's he mumbling about?"

"Don't know. He doesn't make himself understood, see? He looks like he's having a breakdown or somethin'. We haven't had any job offers either. Maybe that's his problem. And we might be evicted any day. Hell, I'm gloomy meself. What do I do? Huh, Sarge? I sure would like to help old Kev."

"I don't know. Nervous upsets are not something in my experience. Send him to a priest."

"I tried that, but he looked absolutely horrified at the suggestion. It's not like we was regular church goers, you know."

"Like I said, this is an unknown area for me."

"Could you talk to him?"

"Look, I can't bring back Boylan, or your jobs, or save you from eventual eviction, so what could I say to him except, 'Buck up, things'l get better'? That would probably just get me a sneer."

Duffy looked crestfallen. "Thanks for listenin' anyway."

"I'll ask around if anyone needs bodyguards or errand runners, but remember, I ain't into local politics the way you two were. Ask Bathhouse John. He's feeling upbeat now that he's goin' to be an alderman. Or ask Hinky Dink."

"That's an idea." Duffy seemed a bit less morose.

"You can't wait for a job to be handed to you by some fairy godfather. You've got to go out huntin'. Meanwhile, I've got a job of me own to do." And with that he headed back into the rooms once occupied by Mrs. Plotz.

The two rooms, the kitchen and her sleeping quarters, were as he'd last seen them, minus her body. *The bedroom is probably the only place I can find anything. Hate goin' through her clothes especially her unmentionables.* Nevertheless, he

proceeded to do just that; after which, he tackled
an impressive pile of newspapers and books. The
Abendpost, among several other Chicago dailies,
were on a table near the bed. No wonder the
woman could complain about the state of things
politically. I'm thinkin' there was more to her
then Weber and I thought.

And the books. In German. I need Weber to
translate the titles. Jaysus, *Brueder Karamazov,*
that one I know. It could only be The Brothers
Karamazov. He gave a whistle. He'd read the
book himself in English translation. He was very
impressed. *But I need to talk to Henry.*

Going back into the saloon, he asked Sloan if
Henry was available.

"Sure is. Let me call him." After a few
minutes, the old fellow appeared.

"Listen Henry, come to Mrs. Plotz's rooms
with me. I need some things explained." Once
there and seated, Mike described the newspapers
and books he'd seen.

"That's awfully educated readin' matter for
a cook. Can you tell me something more about
her background?"

"Sure. In all her complainin', she said a lot
about her and her husband havin' come down in
the world. Because of politics, they had to leave
the old country where they'd been a lot more
important. Here, they just couldn't seem to get
back their old place in society. Her husband
worked a menial job for the railroad, and she had
to use her cookin' and sewin' skills to help dem
get by. She was edicated. She told me so. Sent
away for all those books through that German

paper she read." Henry scratched his sparsely covered head. "Pretty fat books, must have a lot of smart stuff in 'em. Couldn't read that kind of book meself even if it was in English. But all that readin' just made her grumpy. That's all I know, though."

"Thanks, Henry. I appreciate the info." Mike pressed some coins into Henry's hand. "Have some beers on me. Or does McCarthy let you have them on the house?"

"Ah, Sloan does when McCarthy ain't around." Henry went back to whatever he'd been doing with a grin on his face.

The Brothers Karamazov is about sons wanting their dad out of the way. He gets murdered by one of them. Fathers and sons and a rivalry between old dad and one of the sons over a woman. Something started to foment in Mike's brain, but it was in a very early stage and nothing but a vague hint . . . a mere whisper. He concluded his search with a brief perusal of the kitchen and pantry.

Nothing else turned up and as per the plans made the day before, Mike headed to City Hall eager to talk over the new stuff about Mrs. Plotz with Karl.

"She got killed for some reason. If her murderer is found, just maybe we can find Boylan's killer as well."

In the city hall lobby, he found that besides the pleasant odor of pine, the place was full of elves ho, ho, hoing and jingling bells. *Who decided that politicians deserve this kind of welcome?* Mike shook his head, amused. Upstairs, in front of the squad room stood a well-padded Santa Claus.

"Ah, Sarge, it's me Mulcahy."

"I'd never have guessed. It's disillusioned I am, 'cause here I was thinking it was really Santa. I was going to tell him what I wanted for Christmas."

"Nah, it's just me. And it's collectin' I am. For the public health nurses . . . to get dem fruit and chocolates for all they has to put up with when we haul in bad guys. You know, cursin' anarchists and such, and the poor ladies sometimes get those fellas confused with their own customers." Mike gladly contributed, remembering the swearing and threats in the corridor when Chicago's anarchists had been hauled in after the Traction King's murder.

Entering the squad room, Mike found that Karl had nearly finished the reports. He was grateful as he hated doing paperwork himself. "I've got somethin' interesting to discuss with you." Karl put down his pen, grateful to take a respite.
"

It seems that there was more to old Plotz than we thought. She was an educated woman. The stack of papers in her bedroom indicate a determination to be up on political events."

"How do you know she wasn't just reading the humorous material and the sensational stuff."

"I talked to Henry again. It was politics all right. And get this, she subscribed to that German newspaper of your dad's. She even ordered books through the mail from the paper."

"It's a service my father provides."

"And it wasn't light reading she was doing. Now, I could only make out one title. Listen, Karl, why can't you Germans use good old English writing? German's got all these curliques and fancy flourishes. I couldn't tell an S from an E."

"It's called Gothic, and we're used to it. Maybe some time in the future, we'll change it, but that won't happen for a while."

"Anyway, most were heavy volumes. Both Henry and I were impressed. But the only one I could make out was *The Brothers Karamazov.* You'll have to go to Boylan's and decipher the rest of the titles. It might be helpful. Henry gave me more of her background, and it seems that after they came here, she and her husband never did get back the status they'd had in the old country.

"Now, Karl, you know the story of The Brothers, right?"

"Can't say as I do. I find the Russians a bit heavy. The Germans have plenty of good writers themselves, so do the English, and the French. They're enough for me so far."

"Well, this is a story of a family with a heavy-handed father. His sons mostly resent him. One of them is even his rival over a woman. The old man finally gets done in."

"And your interest in this novel?"

"I just think the book gave Mrs. Plotz some ideas."

"Such as?"

"Father and son relationships."

"Aw, Mike, what's that got to do with Boylan? No one killed him over a woman. We know about his relationships."

"I'm just goin' to let it percolate some more. Somethin' is nudgin' me."

"Keep letting it nudge you if you want. I wouldn't mention it to Steele. It's too vague."

"Oh, and Duffy was in Sloan's. It seems Kevin is havin' some sort of breakdown. Sounds like he's going to pieces and Duffy's concerned."

"That's their problem. Oh, and I did send Willie out to hunt down Boylan's lady friend but he hasn't reported back yet." He paused. "Christmas is just a few days away. I've got to get gifts. There'll be all kinds of parties at the various German associations, and frankly, I want to enjoy the season. You do too. I think Steele wouldn't mind if we put everything on the backburner until after the holidays. Christmas is this weekend. We've only got a few more days. Of course you can cogitate all you want, but let's take a rest from all this running around. Maybe thinking about the murders instead of running from pillar to post will be more productive."

Mike finally agreed that was a good plan.

"I can keep from chasin' public transportation for a bit. I've had my fill of stuffed cable cars, slow horse cars, and the smells that go with them."

"Mike, I also think we should make use of the telephone. That way we save a lot of running around."

"And who has a telephone?"

"Boylan's, I bet. Headquarters. Me at my rooming house. The owner charges us and the neighbors for its use and takes messages. She makes a bit extra that way. My parents have a telephone. My father has to be in contact with the newspaper and the newspaper with him. Your aunt's a business woman, she could maybe use one."

Mike thought about it.

"It's ten cents each time. That's a beer and a free lunch. Twice."

"And this is the fellow with a legacy. Come on Mike, it could save you cable fare or an extra long jaunt. It could save you time. Think about that."

Mike still looked dubious about adding telephone numbers to what he already needed to know. He did recognize the growing importance of the telephone. Hell, Chicago already had a book with business numbers listed, called the "yellow pages" from its color. Maybe he'd suggest it to his aunt. After all she was running a business. And come to think of it, it wasn't too convenient going down the street to the grocer's who did have a telephone to make a call.

CHAPTER ELEVEN

Mike and his aunt enjoyed a good Christmas dinner and since they finally got brave enough to light the candles on their first tree, they basked in the ambience of its flickering lights and the scent of pine. Then while his aunt visited elderly neighbors, enjoying bites here and there that she'd actually contributed herself, Mike mulled over what *The Brothers Karamazov* had evoked.

I've got to go back to the Everleigh Club. There's someone that needs to be interviewed again. If Karl thinks it's a wild goose chase, I'll go alone. He laughed. *I'll give him a call. The store down the street has a phone, and it's good for business to let customers pay to use it as a convenience.* And it did save the two men time. They agreed to meet at the Everleigh Club. Mike felt quite clever, because he'd called the Club first to see if Daisy was there. *Karl's right, the telephone has definite possibilities.*

Ada and Minna Everleigh were again pleased to have Sergeants Weber and Rafferty in their establishment. Being on the side of law and order, after usually being denounced by civic groups as contributing to vice and crime, they were happy once again to aid in possibly resolving Alderman's Boylan's murder. The sisters had set aside a room near the pantry and kitchens where Daisy could be quizzed in private. Even coffee and a selection of savory treats were provided. At first timid, but warming under their gentle questioning and the offer of coffee and treats, Daisy seemed eager to help them. Both men looked at her sympathetically. They weren't that far removed from those who had to work hard to get by. She was obviously shy about her appearance and tried to hide her work-reddened hands under her apron.

"Daisy, we have questions about Kevin. Remember we spoke of his background last time and you gave us some particulars. Now his friend Duffy, you remember him?" She nodded. "He's become quite anxious about his friend. He thinks the young man is having a breakdown of some sort and sought our advice. Perhaps if we knew still more about his mother and his childhood we could render more aid." Daisy nodded agreement with this plea from Rafferty.

"Just go over his background again and add more detail than you did the last time. For instance, we know she conceived when in the employ of Toots Sweeney, who acted like a good Christian should and offered her work when she could have very easily thrown her out into the streets."

Daisy nodded, "Toots Sweeny treated all of us decent, not like some of those wicked madams and pimps. She was more like the Everleighs, but not as good in business. Ain't Ada and Minna Everleigh clever?"

"Yes, they surely are. Now to get back to Kevin. You said he was a sort of mascot for the ladies and grew up there at Sweeney's place. Then that Alderman Boylan heard of the tyke and his mother and offered to send him to a nearby parochial school and paid the tuition until he was about thirteen. Did he board out?"

"Sometimes, but he also came home to Sweeny's at holidays and such. Didn't seem to fit in anymore. Couldn't seem to cozy up to his mum either after a few years. She could see he disrespected her then. She tried to make up for that and said she really did know who his father was and that their getting together was a lovin' relationship. I'm afraid she hinted that Boylan was his dad.

"Earlier when she named him Kevin Fitzpatrick, we figured it was because her bein' a Catholic that she was mentionin' St. Patrick. Now suddenly she's hinting it's Boylan. And his payin' for the school. That helped put that over. You could see Kevin liked that idea. But the rest of us knowed it wasn't true as the Alderman never ever came to Toots Sweeny for anything. We knowed that now and then if he heard of some Irish Catholic havin' a hard time, why, he did a bit of charity. As well he should, him being a man with lots of money." Daisy leaned back after her long speech. Weber quickly offered her more coffee and more of cheese and savory tarts that had been made available as well.

"Can you add anything, Daisy? How about when Kevin was older?"

"Well, we knowed that the school must have given Alderman Boylan a good report 'cause he took Kevin on as an errand runner. So did Toots. Then later, he gets to be Boylan's bodyguard along with Duffy. By that time, Kevin was sort of avoiding his mum. Saw her as little as possible, I think."

"Do you see what I'm getting at here, Karl?" Rafferty asked.

"That doesn't add up to murder," Karl replied in a low voice. To Daisy, he said, "You've been a big help, and I guess we will let you get back to work for now, but if you remember anything else, let one of the Everleighs know and they'll contact us. With your information we'll be able to do something for Kevin. Meanwhile, why don't you take the rest of these savories for yourself," though Karl reached for one last sausage.

She quickly whisked out a handkerchief and packed them up. "You two are real gentlmen."

"Now," added Rafferty, "I believe we'd like to interview that lass with the raven hair, Miss Evangelina, who was a favorite with Boylan. She might tell us his thoughts on Kevin. Is she available?"

"She must be. They'll all be gettin' up now from their beauty sleeps. And she sure does have the most beautiful hair, so dark and silky with just the right amount of curl. She's nice too, always has a kind word for others. Let me ask if she can come and see you."

"Look, Mike, you saw how broken up Kevin was."

"Was he? That may also have been an act. A kid in his circumstances has to put up a good front for example. Can you imagine what a raggin' he would have gotten in school if the other kids had known his origins? He wouldn't have survived. Lettin' not much show of your inner feelings but also playacting when the situation calls for it. I think our Kevin is like that.

"And what about now? Is that playacting?"

"Well, two murders might well cause some sort of breakdown. Moreover, he's just the sort of person Mrs. Plotz might reasonably have allowed into her presence, thinkin' she had nothing to worry about."

We've got no other line of inquiry so we might as well go with your notion of an aggrieved Kevin. Though why suddenly attack Boylan?"

"That's what we have to find out."

Evangelina tried to help. "But really, Alderman Boylan never said anything about either Kevin or Brian Duffy. He'd sooner tell me Irish fairy tales. And good he was at it too. Puttin' on all sorts of voices. He could be scary or funny." She sighed. "I miss him." She touched the large green bow on the top of her head. "He give me this last St. Patrick's day. Said I could be

Irish for the day. Give me a shamrock too." She
started to tear up. "He wasn't just after sex. He
was a mentor too. With Miss Minna's permission
he invested some of my money. I've even got me
a bank book to prove it was multiplyin'." Now
the tears became a gusher. She rose abruptly,
"I'm so sorry."

The men were both surprised at her outburst.
She was acting like she'd lost someone special,
and she evidently had.

"Sorry," she repeated and left the room, a
handkerchief to her eyes.

"I keep meeting different Boylans," ventured
Mike. "And here's another. The mentor. I've
already met the hard-nosed saloon keeper and
gambling impresario, the alderman looking out
for his constituents and the man enriching
himself on boodle. He cheated on his wife but
left his mistresses with kindly thoughts or at least
with furniture and linens. A good Irishman, but
not a man given to blowing up Brits. None of that
Clan na Gael stuff for him. And there's also the
doer of good deeds . . . including my legacy."

"What's that old saying, Mike? About the
good in the worst of us and the bad in the best of
us. I guess hardly anyone is all one thing or
another. But where does all this leave the two of
us as regards the murder? That's what we should
be trying to solve." Both men sat in silence for
what seemed a long time until Mike returned to
his recent suspicions about Kevin.

"You know, Kevin always seems to have

given me the cold shoulder. As if he was jealous
of any attention Boylan paid me. I wonder if I
can make him take some overt action against me
if I challenged him in some way." Weber looked
doubtful. "I could say I needed to question him.
And where better than in Boylan's own private
room at the saloon. Maybe I'll come right out
with an accusation."

"What exactly have you got? You know that
Kevin probably thought Boylan was his dad.
That's something he might be desperate to hang
onto. So why shoot him?"

"But suppose Kevin wanted Boylan to
acknowledge him openly and Boylan laughed at
him."

"I don't know, Mike. This sounds like one of
those Gothic plots my sister's always reading.
And wouldn't Boylan be kinder than that."

"Well, pity's hard to take too. Anyway, we
need to be checking in with Willie and finding
out about Boylan's first full-time lady friend. If
that comes to nothing, we can get back to
Kevin."

A phone call to headquarters made from the
Everleigh Club found Willie had returned from
his investigation. Over the telephone, he
informed them that it was a dead end. The lady
and Boylan had tired of one another. She split
with a gift of cash which she wisely invested in
her own rooming house, figuring her days in the
chorus line were over. She makes a grand
landlady, according to Willie and is engaged to
one of her tenants. No grudge there.

"So it's back to Kevin. You know, I could

throw up to him that Boylan left me a legacy just because of our long-time Irish connection. And the fact that Kevin was only an employee ought to be enough to tell him he was no relation to Boylan."

"In other words you hope he explodes."

"With you and Willie and others close by."

"You realize that if he was really putting on an act, he may still have his Colt." Mike acknowledged that possibility.

"This is going to have to be carefully set up, and we'll need Steele's permission."

Mike agreed and added, "I just want these damn murders solved and to put the whole mess behind us."

Steele shrugged at the latest theory.

"What the hell! There's nothing else. Give it a try, but for God's sake, be careful. When you finalize your scheme, run it by me again. At least right now, there's no other important murder to get our attention, just the usual domestics and gang shootings. These complicated ones . . . well, we sure can do without those."

Karl and Mike and at least some of their colleagues, including the recently returned Willie, sat down and tried to work out a scenario to trap Fitzpatrick. They weren't even sure if he'd take the bait. Though Mike counted on the fact that when he and Karl had ordered Kevin and Brian Duffy around the last few weeks, they always seemed to want to be on the right side of the law.

Mike and Karl went to Boylan's to look over the premises once more.

"How's he going to get in? If he's worried what this whole meeting's about, he'll not be wanting to come in through the saloon," Karl pointed out.

"I'll just tell him the doors are open through the old gambling house and that he can come right over to Boylan's private room."

"I just hope that doesn't give him any ideas about getting even with you and thinking he can get away with it."

"Aw, of course, he'll be suspicious. I mean, wouldn't you be?"

Karl was still dubious. "Let's just hope he's crazy enough to go for it. It won't work if he's a cool customer."

"Remember what Duffy said, that he's on the edge. I'm giving him a shove."

"Remember, Mike, all that remorse, that play acting about tossing the gun? That shows a man who's able to deceive, to put on an imposture. It shows a man clever at covering his tracks."

Matters were arranged. Sloan knew something was going on but was told to mind his own business which he was more than happy to do. And McCarthy couldn't at this point have cared less. All he wanted was to get rid of Boylan's saloon, gambling houses, and hopefully still turn a profit. He rarely looked into the business any more except to pick up any monies that keeping the saloon open still managed to attract.

Duffy was told about the meeting, but he was led to assume that Rafferty was going to work some magic and make Kevin tip top again. The invitation to Fitzpatrick was by telephone. His hotel had a phone and Mike was now a complete convert to its usefulness. He was preemptory in demanding Kevin's attendance insisting that the two of them had matters to clarify about their relationships to Boylan. Kevin grumbled but said he'd show up. Mike's allies, including Karl and Willie, arrived much earlier than the appointed time of seven o'clock and situated themselves close by. Some were set up down in the kitchen which wasn't far away. It had certainly been too close for Mrs. Plotz. Karl was actually in Boylan's room behind a screen, backing up against the wall. Only one lamp was lit and that allowed the periphery of the room to remain in the shadows.

Mike sat at the table, a lamp on a stand behind him. His pistol was handy in his pocket. The whole scheme was now beginning to make him feel like an actor in some silly little play. He didn't know if he could even pull it off. The waiting began to wear on him. He thought he heard the creaking of someone approaching, but it was much too soon. Whispering to himself, "I'll be hearing the flappin' of sheets next and feelin' strange drafts. What's next Mike," he asked himself, "moans and clanking? Ghosts do get in their hauntin' in the night."

To his relief there was at last a knock on the
door. He called out, Kevin answered, and Mike
told him to come in. He began his verbal assault
immediately.

"Well, Kevin, you and I, there's always been
something between us since we first met. You've
always shown me resentment, that is, when I had
Boylan's attention. Jealous is what you were.
And now I know why. We've been hearing from
folks who knew you from a long time ago. They
got the impression that you believe you were
Boylan's flesh and blood. I know you got that
notion from your mother, a bit belatedly, since
she only started feeding you that blather when
she saw herself losing any affection you may
ever have had for her. And that, as a result of
Boylan's misplaced charity for an Irish tyke born
in a whorehouse.

"You ain't anymore Boylan's son than I am.
He's done a lot more for me though. Left me a
hefty legacy, he did, in his will. But you were
never anything but an errand boy or bodyguard.
That wasn't enough for you though, was it?
Feeling deprived, were you?

Kevin began to rock back and forth and his
expression was anything but calm. His agitation
was becoming obvious. Some of what I'm saying
must be getting through, Mike thought.

"You shot him. Why? Did he laugh at your
fantasy? Or maybe he felt sorry for you for
believing such a fairy tale. You couldn't take it

and killed the man. Oh, I'm sure it wasn't premeditated. A spur of the moment thing. Only it had consequences, didn't it? Mrs. Plotz heard something and she approached you. So you did for her as well. Well, the chickens are now coming home to roost, Kev. Your fantasy is a bust."

At that Kevin, seemed almost literally to blow apart. Out came the Colt which had obviously never gone into Bubbly Creek. In a shaking hand, he tried to bring it to bear on Mike, who instantly pushed over the table, and using it as a shield, drew his own weapon. In the corner of his eye he saw the screen toppling and Karl take a dive for Kevin. As a result his shots went wild, but he keep firing until he'd been subdued by both men and the gun wrestled from his hand.

Finally, handcuffed and sitting on the floor, all the rage seemed to go out of him. By this time, Willie and the others were in the room as well. "That's a confession as far as I'm concerned. Come on, Kev, did Boylan laugh at you?"

Kevin sighed, "He did, briefly, then when he saw what it was doin' to me--'Poor kid', 'Oh, you poor kid.' I didn't want his pity. I wanted him to acknowledge me as his son. He was coverin' up his own wrongdoing by ignoring me. He pretended. He is my father. Mrs. Plotz knew it. She said as much when we met. She felt sorry for me. Said fathers and sons often had these antagonisms, wanted to know if we was rivals over some woman. Stupid old bitch. Said she needed help to set up someplace, with a friend she sez, and would I help her with some money."

"Which you really didn't have, right?" asked Karl. "How did she get in touch with you?'

"She left a note or sent a note to the hotel. Bastard on the desk had a laugh about my lady friend. And nah, I didn't have but a bit, and she sez she needs more and surely with Boylan being my papa, he must have given me plenty. Said I was always well turned out. Hell, that's where the money I earned went. Boylan's son has to look good. Greedy old besom. Up with muscle aches that night, she sez, and she heard me and Boylan raising our voices, stepped out of the kitchen and saw me leave. Had heard the gun go off too."

Mike sneered at that remark, "As if it were an accidental discharge. And later, of course, a cast iron pan was handy."

"She knew I was Boylan's son. I feel bad about her and Boylan. She believed me."

"You sure did put on a good show of feeling bad, but you kept the gun, didn't you?"

"I needed it. Didn't I? Had you to worry about, didn't I?" He sneered at Mike and looked defiantly around the room at the other detectives who'd been dealing with those coming from the saloon wanting to know what was going on even though they'd been warned not to butt in if they heard any noise from upstairs.

"It's time to call the police van," said Mike, now weary and wanting nothing more than to get the whole mess shifted to headquarters and to get shut of it himself. He wanted the whole sad business finished. "I'm not celebratin'. Karl it's a sorry mess, it is.

"Look, Mike, in some ways, yes, I feel sorry for Kevin. But he did kill two people and cover it up pretty neatly. Yeah, life shorted him. A kid born in a whorehouse, but at some point he has to accept responsibility for what got into him. Boylan's the innocent party here, don't forget that."

"Believe me, I'm not." But Mike still looked dejected, not so much about Kevin as about the unnecessary death of Boylan.

"Come on, it's Christmas time. Take on some of the season's cheer. Anyway, we've got to report to Steele. He'll be thankful it all went well. You know he was dubious about it."

"Yeah, yeah, I know. Let the police van leave. I don't want to sit and stare at Kevin. I'll see him again anyway. We can get there by cable car. It'll take longer and give me time to settle down." Karl agreed.

By the time they reached City Hall and the detective bureau, Steele had already been appraised of what had happened. He stepped out of his office to congratulate them, especially Rafferty. "But something else has come up, and it's of interest to you both, but especially you, Weber."

He preceded them into the office and then motioned to them to be seated.

"This is old business, fellas. You remember Mr. Smithson, Purcell's business manager?" They both nodded. "Well, he dropped in to see me." Now they both looked concerned. "No, no, nothing much has changed. But he did bring something that I think would interest you. He's still scrutinizing all the financial records that passed through Fielding's hands. At that time he already had doubts that everything wasn't on the up and up."

"So the man was cookin' the books?" asked Rafferty.

"Not so it was easily noticed. But he did take advantage of his position. Smithson finally located a small ledger hidden at the back of some ordinary and innocent files. Fielding was nipping a bit here and there for his own purposes, and he kept accounts. I'll read you about some of them. It seems the firm was paying for some debts he ran up at the Everleigh Club."

"That damn Fielding! That skunk!" burst out an indignant Weber. "An abuser and cheating on his wife as well." He paused. "I didn't think the sisters let debts run up."

"They probably don't. But it wasn't a large sum and he was Purcell's nephew. They probably suspected he'd be eager to pay up, not wishing to let his uncle know what he was up to. He also paid gambling debts to Boylan's out of company money. At least, the figures shown were large enough so they were certainly not a saloon tab."

"His uncle presumably would not have been happy to know this was goin' on," offered Rafferty.

"But it's another entry that may be of greater interest to you two, especially you, Karl. It's labeled 'for the extermination of a pest' and the nib of the pen was pressed so hard into the paper it almost went through. Smithson gave me the original and made himself a copy." He handed it over to Weber. "Are you thinking what I thought when I read it?"

"If I read you correctly, that pest was me. The bastard hired some thug to shoot me. That damned matter has been in the back of my mind since it happened. All this time I was still seeing some shooter down dark alleys or behind a bush. Look, Mike, fifty bucks he paid someone. Damn him."

"Now I'm not saying 100 percent that this is what the entry is really about but the idea sure occurred to me the minute I saw it and I didn't think it referred to termite control."

"Me neither," agreed Weber. Rafferty also concurred.

"Let's hope you can rest easier now. Smithson probably didn't make that connection but wanted to show me Fielding's other failings. I'll hang on to it but the fellow's locked up and this will probably just be between the three of us."

"It's certainly a load off my mind. And if there's a chance someone else is out there . . .? I don't think so or why hasn't there been another attempt since then.

Your holidays can be more peaceful, eh?" Weber nodded. "Now the two of you go and do your paperwork on Kevin."

As the two men stepped into the outer office, Mike commented, "I'll need to let Duffy know about Kevin's arrest and confession. He'll be plenty upset. I think he genuinely liked the kid."

Several days later, Mike told Karl about his meeting with Duffy.

"You should have seen Duffy when I told him. He kept sayin', 'It ain't possible! It ain't possible! I didn't even know all that shite!' He looked like he'd been hit over the head with a barge pole.

"And he sez, 'Just when Hinky Dink offered to take us on. We would of had us steady jobs with a decent employer. Ah, hell,' he sez! I felt sorry for Duffy. He liked workin' for Boylan and he liked workin' with Kevin. That's enough of that." He sat down looking deflated.

"What are you doing with your time off?" asked Karl, hoping to get Mike on a more cheerful subject.

"Spendin' it with Aunt Maggie, I suppose. She'll be making a feast again. Turkey probably. Still, me aunt will be sharing the leftovers with poorer neighbors, so at least we won't be eating turkey made eight different ways for two weeks." Mike didn't seem much elated by the prospect of the future feast.

"What you need is a sweetheart. I'll bet some of those helpers your aunt employs would consider you a good catch."

"They're older than I am for God's sake. Drop the subject. Stop match-making."

Weber took the advice lest he make Mike even gloomier. "Well, be thankful at least that we have some time off. You can unwind from the Boylan business and look forward to smaller problems in 1893. And the Fair's coming. That's going to be interesting."

Mike rose, "I got a lot of thinkin' to do. There are sure a lot of sides to people, aren't there? Good and bad. I guess I won't be makin' such simple judgments in the future. We're all a lot more complicated." After a thoughtful pause, he said, "I guess I might else well be on my way. I suppose you'll be having Christmas with your family. Give them my best wishes for the day," Mike called back as he left.

Karl was a bit broody himself. He hadn't heard from Caroline and he'd thought for sure they'd see each other at least once over the holidays. Both men got a boost later in the day. When Karl arrived at his rooming house, there was a letter waiting, an invitation to see Caroline and Mrs. Purcell and her daughters as well. In a considerably brighter mood, he began thinking about gifts. "I'll have to hustle and get some flowers and chocolates for the ladies." He spent the evening cheerfully envisioning happy scenes now, not only with his family but another also very dear to him.

In the meantime, when Mike arrived at home, his aunt presented him with a Christmas card.

"Now who's that from, Michael?"

With a big grin plastered across his face, Mike was able to admit it was from Gretel, Karl's sister.

"Why, how very forward of her to send you a card. Did you send her one first?" Mike shook his head. "Well, she is certainly a bold one."

"She's a modern young lady, and I'm sure glad she is. I'm going to get her one and post it straight away. I'm glad she's got more nerve than I have." Christmas was suddenly looking brighter. He could actually imagine holding hands and maybe, just maybe, in time, planting a kiss on that lovely face. Those thoughts wiped away more serious ponderings, thoughts of Boylan and Kevin Fitzgerald and put him in a much better frame of mind for Christmas.

Glossary

Ancient Order of Hibernians An Irish Catholic fraternal organization founded in 1836 to assist the Irish who faced discrimination in the United States.

Blind Pigs Ilicit establishments that sold liquor. They usually drew folks with less money but would nevertheless have been a blot on the scene when Chicago was trying to impress visitors to the World's Columbian Exposition.

Boodle A bribe or other illicit payment, especially to or from a politician but to others as well, the police for example.

Clan na Gael An Irish organization in the United States in the late nineteenth century that aggressively acted in the interests of an independent Ireland.

Dunne, Peter Finley Journalist and humorist. His fame rests on Martin Dooley, an imaginary Irish saloonkeeper on Chicago's West Side. He reviewed public men and affairs with wit and wisdom and that made him a national institution. Even though he teased Teddy Roosevelt, Roosevelt nonetheless enjoyed reading his articles.

Everleigh Club Most famous bordello in Chicago. It also had a national reputation and hosted foreign nobility as well as Gentleman Jim Corbett, Bet-a-Million Gates and others. It was run by two sisters, Ada and Minna Everleigh and was well protected by both important local politicians and, for a bit of boodle, some local police as well.

Foy, Eddie Popular Irish entertainer-manager of the era.

Levee This was the red light district from the1880s until it was finally shut down in the early twentieth century. It covered an area of four blocks (see map on page 4) in Chicago's South Loop between 18th and 22nd. It was part of the First Ward which contained many brothels including the famous Everleigh Club), panel houses, saloons, and dance halls.

Panel Houses Panel houses were the invention of thieves of both sexes. Victims were lured into a room by a woman. The victim is told to lock the door himself and it is still locked when he wakens but he is minus his money. He has been watched by accomplices through carefully concealed holes. There may be sliding panels that can be moved or the lock can be worked from the outside. The woman is still there beside the man in a supposedly locked room and she has no money. The victim can, therefore, sometimes be induced to believe that he was robbed before he entered the place, and he goes away without complaining to the police.

Note: This book is a work of fiction though it features some real historic personages, events and places. The plot required that these folk and especially the Everleigh Club start their careers a bit earlier than actually happened. However, they most probably would have appreciated having these additional years of fun and profit.

Made in the USA
Columbia, SC
13 September 2020